PENGUIN BOOKS

... writers in ...mporar... ...born in 1954 and ...t up in Suss... After leaving school ... began training as a journalist. He then had occasiona... ...bs, mainly in the building industry. Melvin started wri...ing in his twenties and wrote on and off for fifteen years before having his first book, *The Cry of the Wolf*, published in 1990. In 1997 his controversial bestseller *Junk* won the Guardian Children's Fiction Award and the Carnegie Medal. It was also shortlisted for the 1998 Whitbread Children's Book of the Year. His book *Doing It* won the LA Times Young People's Book of the Year Award in 2004. Four of his novels have been shortlisted for the Carnegie Medal: *The Cry of the Wolf*, *An Angel for May*, *The Baby and Fly Pie* and *The Ghost Behind the Wall*. Melvin now writes full-time and lives in Hebden Bridge with his partner, Anita.

Books by Melvin Burgess

Bloodsong

Bloodtide

Burning Issy

The Cry of the Wolf

Doing It

Junk

Kite

Lady: My Life as a Bitch

Loving April

Nicholas Dane

Sara's Face

Tiger Tiger

For younger readers

An Angel for May

The Baby and Fly Pie

The Earth Giant

The Ghost Behind the Wall

MELVIN BURGESS

KILL ALL ENEMIES

PENGUIN BOOKS

PENGUIN BOOKS

Published by the Penguin Group
Penguin Books Ltd, 80 Strand, London WC2R ORL, England
Penguin Group (USA) Inc., 375 Hudson Street, New York, New York 10014, USA
Penguin Group (Canada), 90 Eglinton Avenue East, Suite 700, Toronto, Ontario, Canada M4P 2Y3
(a division of Pearson Penguin Canada Inc.)
Penguin Ireland, 25 St Stephen's Green, Dublin 2, Ireland (a division of Penguin Books Ltd)
Penguin Group (Australia), 250 Camberwell Road, Camberwell, Victoria 3124, Australia
(a division of Pearson Australia Group Pty Ltd)
Penguin Books India Pvt Ltd, 11 Community Centre, Panchsheel Park, New Delhi – 110 017, India
Penguin Group (NZ), 67 Apollo Drive, Rosedale, Auckland 0632, New Zealand
(a division of Pearson New Zealand Ltd)
Penguin Books (South Africa) (Pty) Ltd, 24 Sturdee Avenue, Rosebank, Johannesburg 2196, South Africa

Penguin Books Ltd, Registered Offices: 80 Strand, London WC2R ORL, England

penguin.com

First published 2011
001 – 10 9 8 7 6 5 4 3 2 1

Set in 12/14.5 pt Bembo Book MT Std
Typeset by Palimpsest Book Production Limited, Falkirk, Stirlingshire
Printed in Great Britain by Clays Ltd, St Ives plc

British Library Cataloguing in Publication Data
A CIP catalogue record for this book is available from the British Library

ISBN: 978–0–141–33564–3

www.greenpenguin.co.uk

Penguin Books is committed to a sustainable future for our business, our readers and our planet. This book is made from paper certified by the Forest Stewardship Council.

For Anita

Contents

PART I

School

Billie

I'd been good for nearly a week. Only one fight; it must have been a record for me. I should have known it couldn't last.

I was walking across the car park by the pub on the corner with Riley and his gang, when one of them spotted Rob walking towards us. I knew something was going to happen. Rob's that sort of kid. He wasn't doing anything – he didn't have to. He was just wrong. Everything about him was wrong. Wrong shape, wrong clothes. Wrong ears. Yeah, you heard, wrong ears.

'Look at the state of that,' said Riley. 'What a moron. Look at his ears.'

'What do you care about his ears?' I asked. I was genuinely interested. I mean – ears?

'I'll show you,' said Riley. 'Oi! Robbie,' he said, grabbing hold of him. He whipped an arm over Rob's neck and got him in a head lock.

I'd just been chucked out of the Brant the week before and I was doing everything I could to stay out of trouble. Hey, I'd even got myself some new mates. Hannah at the Brant said I needed some mates. OK, it was only Riley and his crooked little gang of thugs. But I was doing it, wasn't I? Socializing. Being one of a crowd.

And then I have to stand there watching them bully this fat kid because they don't like the shape of his ears.

Normally I'd have blown a fuse, but this time I just stood there and watched. I thought, *It's none of your business, Billie. Just leave it. They're not going to kill him. It's only pain.*

That's one of Hannah's. When I asked her what to do if someone started on me, she said, 'They're not going to kill you. Take it and walk away. It's only pain.' And this wasn't even my pain. It was just one more fat kid getting pushed around.

I stood and watched. I didn't turn a hair.

Riley had Rob's head under his arm, and he was rubbing his ears, hard. And Rob was going, 'Ow ow ow!' like an idiot, and his ears were getting redder and redder and someone else was behind kicking him up the arse. It was none of my business. I was just watching. I'm a good girl, me. Then Riley walked over with Rob's head under his arm and he said, 'Go on, Billie. You have a go. Give 'em a rub.'

I just said, 'You want me to have a go?'

'Yeah,' said Riley.

'How about this?' I said. So I punched him right on the nose. *Bang*. Down went Riley. Then – in with the boot. *Bang bang bang*. And then his girlfriend, Jess or whatever her name is, came and tried it on, so I did her – *bang!* – just once, in the teeth. Down she goes, blood everywhere.

'I don't do bullies,' I said. And I walked off – just in time to see the bus going past. All along the windows a row of faces turned to watch me.

Can you believe me? In public. Right in front of anyone who cared to see. I am so stupid!

I turned my face away and headed off, out of the car park. Then behind me – 'Billie . . . wait . . . Billie . . .'

Jesus.

Rob's all right. He was a new kid too, not as new as me – I'd only been there a week – but he hadn't been there long. Just long enough to arrive right at the bottom of the pecking order. We'd had a bit of a chat, talked about music and stuff like that. But I wasn't in the mood for him just then.

He caught up with me. 'Thanks . . . thanks . . . That was . . . that was . . .' He was all out of breath, bending over, trying to get the words out.

'Don't,' I said.

'What?'

'Just don't. You and your bloody ears.'

'What about my ears?'

'They stick out. If it wasn't for your bloody ears, I wouldn't have had to do that.'

'I'll change 'em for you.'

'What?'

'I've got a spare pair at home.'

'What?'

'Joke.' He smiled at me. 'You know.'

I turned and walked off, but he wasn't giving up. He came running after me.

'I just wanted to say thanks.'

'You said it.'

'We could be mates,' he said.

I turned to look at him. 'What are you on?' I said.

'Why not?' he said.

'People like me don't make friends with people like you.'

'Why?'

'Because all people like you want is for people like me to sort your fights out for you.'

'I can fight me own fights, thanks.'

'Yeah, it looks like it.'

'No, but you're new. I'm new. We could hang out together.'

'Look. I can't afford to have fights,' I told him. 'I'm on my last chance. I told you. I've been through five schools in the past two years. I even got chucked out of the Brant, and they like me there. Statside is the last school that'll have me. If I blow this, it's the LOK. I can't do the LOK. Do you know the LOK?'

'No.'

'It's this terrible place. I'm not doing the LOK for anyone.'

No way. I already got sent there once. I lasted one day and I was banging at the door of the Brant, begging them to let me back in. It's evil. They have guards with batons patrolling the corridors. They lock the doors behind you everywhere you go. You have to have an escort even just to go to the toilet. It's full of nutters. Just because I like fighting, that doesn't make me a nutter.

'You don't have to go to the LOK,' he said. 'Don't fight. I'll show you how. It's easy. You just get beat up.' He smiled at me again.

I laughed. 'Yeah, I'm not very good at that,' I told him. I had another look at him. He was one of those kids. Overweight and bouncing about like a puppy dog. He didn't give up easy, though.

'Look at the state of you,' I said. 'You're the sort of kid who gets picked on all the time. It'd be fights all day and all night if I was friends with you.'

'We can be friends out of school, then.'

I shook my head. I was thinking about something else Hannah always said. 'Trouble with you, Billie, is,' she said, 'you always make the wrong sort of friends. None of 'em last, none of them are ever there for you. Why don't you get with someone nice for a change?'

Yeah, great – but how do you know? I can never tell whether they're just after something or if they really want to be mates. I had a good look at Rob and tried to work it out. I hadn't got a clue.

'I'll think about it,' I said.

'Yesssss!' he hissed. And that made me smile.

He walked with me to the bus stop. I wasn't going to the usual one because I had a visit to make. Once I decided to let him, I quite liked him being there. Maybe he was a nice kid – why not?

'I won't let you down, Billie,' he said. 'I'll be a good friend.'

Yeah, right, I thought. *We'll see.*

Chris

It wasn't me who started it this time, it was Alex.

Monday morning. We were humming.

I know, I know. It's not the teacher's fault that no one in the past two hundred years has been even remotely interested in what they're on about. It's school. It's boring. But they could make an effort. Look at Mrs Connelly who does English. I mean, books by dead people are only marginally more interesting than the cross section of dead frog skin Mr Wikes was drawing on the board, but at least she tries. But this was science. This was Mr Wikes, the most boring man in the known universe, whose idea of education was to stand with his back to you and draw on the board.

That's not education. It's fraud. If it wasn't kids he was torturing, he'd be put on trial.

It can do you damage, boredom at those levels. On the Chris Trent bored-ometer, anyone going over 100 needs to be taken out of class and put to work counting nuts. After 200, the learning process goes into reverse. At 300, your reflection in the mirror starts to age and you lose the ability to digest pizza. At 500, your brain begins to eat itself.

Wikes scores several thousand regularly. So, really, I was humming for the sake of my health.

The point about humming is they can't tell who it is. Wikes spends a few minutes pretending it's not happening before he turns round and sneaks a look, but of course all he sees is kids, heads down, writing away. If he had any sense he'd keep his trap shut – it's about the only time anyone actually does any work in his class. He can't help himself, though. It's not enough to be bored, see – you have to be bored in silence.

'All right, you lot, you can stop it now, thank you,' he said tiredly, before turning back to the board and carrying on as if nothing had happened. It's just a front, though. Inside he's a seething mass of resentment and rage. He was on a good day this time – he must have managed at least five minutes before he finally erupted. The marker pen went flying and he leaped away from the board, slavering like a bison in rut.

'Right! That's enough! Who is it? Stop that noise! Who's making that noise?' he yelled. It's quite a sight, the Wikes in full territorial display. He froths. It's a form of scent marking. You can get sprayed if you sit too close.

'Not me, sir . . . I'm not, sir . . . It's not *me* . . .' everyone goes. Of course, when one person speaks the others are still humming so the noise levels remain exactly the same.

When it finally dawns on him that tantrums won't

work, Wikes tries *cunning*. Mistake. He strolls casually up and down the rows leaning slightly to one side. If he gets too close, all you have to do is stop and the humming carries on a metre or so ahead of him. It's like watching a dog chasing its own tail.

Then he strikes.

WIKES	[*Speaking very quickly and suddenly*] Chris, how are you today?
CHRIS (that's me)	[*Equally quickly*] Very well, thank you, sir, and how are you?
WIKES	Fine, thank you . . .

The humming goes all wobbly at this point as people try not to laugh out loud, so then Wikes loses it totally. 'Stop it! Stop! You – you! I know it's you!'

That's me. As usual. He pounces and hoiks me out of my seat, yelling and spitting.

'Out! Out! Get out of my class!'

'OK! Get off me.'

It's funny, but – he has no business shoving me like that. He's got to pick on someone, I suppose, but why is it always me? Out I go, slam the door on him. He opens it and creeps after me, growling like an enraged lemming.

'You will go straight to the headmaster and tell him what you've done.'

Then he slams the door on me. And that's that.

I didn't go and see the head, of course. Wikes *might* ask him about it, but he probably won't. It's humiliating for the teacher to have to send someone to see senior management. It's like they're saying, 'Help me! I can't cope!' Which of course, in Wikes's case, they can't.

It was the last lesson of the day. I could have headed off home, but I didn't want to be seen leaving school, so I headed off to the hall instead. No one goes backstage unless there's a play on. There's this little room where they keep all the gels and the old costumes and stuff. No one ever disturbs you there.

I sat down on a wicker trunk of old costumes and chewed some gum. I'd just about had it with school. They should have let me leave and get on with it, but oh no. You have to stay until your brain melts. Maybe you like sitting in a class with a brain-dead imbecile wondering why Shakespeare used primroses instead of violets to symbolize the end of Hamlet's nose, or finding out how many prime numbers you can stick up a frog's bum before it explodes. Or maybe you're like Alex, and you want to get good grades and go to uni so you can learn how to teach kids to count how many prime numbers, etc. etc. Maybe you just don't have anything better to do. I don't know.

But me? I'm not even going to university. I have better things to do. I'm an entrepreneur, or at least I will be when they start leaving me alone to get on with things. That's how you make money, that's how you get rich, that's how you contribute to society. Not by being a teacher, or a doctor, or by going to uni. By building a business.

I don't want to work for the man. I want to *be* the man.

They can't cope with the fact that actually, instead of being at school, I ought to be out there right now, making my first fortune. They don't do GCSEs in entrepreneuring. Business studies is as near as it gets and that's not very near. I already have a nice little earner on eBay. I know everyone does eBay, but I have a *shop*. I make a profit. £100 last trading month. Not bad! And they think I'd be better off learning how to count up to a million in binary, do they?

I don't think so.

The first bus was full, so me and Alex walked a couple of stops, which is always a pain because you have to go past Statside School, which must be one of the roughest schools in Leeds.

It had been raining. Everything was wet. By the time we got to Statside, most of the kids had already gone, but there were a few still left. The stop was by a church with ivy hanging down an old stone wall on to the street, and the rain must have woken up all the snails that lived there. There were loads of them, crawling all over the place – 'Fat on the flesh of the dear departed,' as Alex pointed out. They were the big brown sort, roving around the pavement with their little faces up in the air and their little horns waving about. It must have been snail heaven at that bus stop because there were dozens of them.

And these two kids were stamping on them.

I mean, OK, I know they're just snails – you don't have to be friends with them. But still. These snails, all they were doing was getting a bit of rain after spending the winter in the wall. It's not much to ask, is it? And then along come two stupid kids who think it's fun stamping on the hapless molluscs so the snail goo goes splat all over the place.

'Leave it out,' I told them.

'What's it to you?' one of the kids said, like I was some kind of perv for watching out for snails. He lifted his foot and got three of them in one go, *splat*, all in a heap. I saw red. I shoved him backwards . . . and then, of course, this vast, fat monster emerged from behind the bus stop where it had been listening to rapists on its iPod and chewing a sackload of pizza crusts or whatever.

'That's my brother,' grunted the monster. I could hear Alex moaning, 'Noooooo.' One of the kids, smirking away, stamped on another snail.

Alex to the rescue. 'Hey, let's go,' he said brightly, scuttling backwards like a rodent.

'Pathetic way to amuse yourself,' I said.

The fat one looked at me.

'It's snails,' he said.

'They're on a day out. Leave 'em alone.'

The little brother lifted up his foot, and 'Cur-runch,' he says, and he did another one in. I stepped forward; he stepped back behind his giant brother and pulled a face at me.

'Enjoy hurting things, do you?' I said.

The fat one shrugged. 'It's snails,' he said again.

Behind him, his little brother reached out a toe and crunched another one. I reached forward to grab him, but the big kid blocked me. The little kid smirked. I went for him again, but Roly Poly pushed me back.

'Leave him alone,' he told me.

'You dribbling furball,' I said.

'Let's go, let's go, let's go,' said Alex from somewhere behind me.

The fat one looked all hurt, as if no one had noticed his furballness before. Not only that but his little brother started sniggering. Result! He didn't have any answer, being a man of little brain, so he crushed a snail instead.

'You quivering gob of dog spit,' I said. The fat one turned red. Everyone laughed. He trod on two snails, one after the other – *crunch*, *crunch*.

It was a trial of nerves. Everyone turned to look at me.

'You farting walrus,' I said.

He crushed another one. The time had come to stop being clever.

'Wanker,' I said.

He cracked.

'Right! That's it,' he shouted. 'You asked for it.' Then he went berserk. He started stamping on all the snails he could find. 'Bang bang bang squelch bang bang!' he screamed, stamping and pulling faces like some kind of overweight Maori on the warpath. He was slithering around on the crushed snails – you could see it was all going to end in disaster. I didn't have to do anything. He looked so ludicrous even his brother hid his face in his hands.

'No, Rob, don't, don't,' he groaned.

And then – the snails got him. All that slimy snail goo. It was bound to happen. His feet shot out one way, his arms another, his fat belly another, his bag yet another. He hung in mid-air for a minute like a elevating hippo . . . then *SPLAT!* Right down on the pavement. Right in the dog shit and the snail corpses, where he belonged.

'Uroerugh,' groaned the fat one.

'The revenge of the snail people is complete,' I said.

And then the bus came along. Perfect! Sometimes, the universe just hands it to you on a plate.

The fat one hauled himself upright just in time to see the bus roll off, with us on it.

'Tosser,' yelled Alex to him, now that it was safe. The fat one didn't say anything. He didn't need to. He just drew his finger across his throat.

We pushed our way upstairs. 'Why'd you do that?' moaned Alex.

'I was saving the snails,' I pointed out.

'I didn't notice many snails getting saved,' said Alex. 'That kid is a psychopath. Did you see the size of him? If him and his family want to squash snails for a hobby, that's fine by me.'

'You're such a chicken,' I said.

Alex scowled. 'It's not being chicken, it's looking

after myself,' he said. 'You could have got punched and you could have got me punched too. It's stupid.'

I shook my head. I mean, we go way back, me and Alex, but . . . Don't get me wrong, I like him. He's OK. But it's like . . . all he ever thinks about is Alex.

'Why are you staring at me?' he asked.

'I was just wondering why we're friends,' I told him.

'We share a similar sense of humour,' he said.

'Oh, yeah, I forgot.'

Alex shook his head. 'Fat lip at twelve o'clock,' he added, changing the subject. This couple got on the bus, a boy and a girl, and the girl had blood on her mouth. He was slouching in front of her, like he was embarrassed to be seen with someone who was bleeding, and she was creeping along behind him, trying not to cry.

Even girls get beaten up at Statside.

They sat down a few seats away. She was trying to mop up with bits of old tissue, the sort of stuff you find rolled up into little twists in your pockets, while he sat there scowling away. I dug out a little packet of tissues I had in my pocket ever since I had a cold a while ago, and I got up to give it to them.

'Here, do you want to use these?' I said. The lad glared at me.

'What's it to you?' he said.

I shook the tissues. 'Do you want them or not?'

He stared at me as if I'd just told him to get stuffed, but the girl reached across and took them.

'Thanks,' she said, and she tossed her head at the bloke like he was being a dick. Which he was.

'No worries,' I said, and I went back to my seat. The lad twisted round to stare at me. What for? Helping his girlfriend? You tell me.

Alex was furious. 'What did you do that for?' he hissed as soon as the lad looked away. 'It's none of your business. What is it with you and violence?'

'Shut up, Alex,' I said.

I looked across at the girl. She'd looked ugly with her bleeding lips, but behind the tissues there was a pretty face, I reckon.

'I wonder what happened to her,' I said.

'Got in a fight with Billie Trevors,' someone said behind us.

I thought, *She's not going to be a looker for long if she gets into trouble with people like that*.

Billie

I was planning on going to see my mum after school but I was so fed up after getting into that fight I was starting to think I might go and see Cookie instead. He's not exactly my boyfriend, but he's the nearest thing I have right now. He works at a burger bar. He's a freak – all he wants is to get pissed and have a grope. I can cope with that; at least you know what you're getting.

But . . . it was Mum's birthday a few days ago. I wanted to see her. I'd got her a present, a nice one. So I thought, *Sod Cookie. I've got more important things to do today*.

I hadn't seen her for ages. She gets depressed. That's what Hannah reckons anyway. Untreated depression, that's what it sounds like to me, she said. I call it untreated being pissed. I didn't even know it was that for a long time. She's a private drinker, my mum. By the time I was ten she was so depressed I couldn't remember what she was like sober.

It crept up gradually with Mum. I was doing more and more about the house. Cleaning, cooking. Doing the shopping on the way home from school. If I didn't do it, we'd all come home and there'd be nothing to eat; she'd've spent it all on booze. By the time I was ten I was getting them up, getting them ready for school, feeding them, doing the washing, keeping the house in order. I was the oldest, see. And then I'd go to school and do a full day there, get the shopping on the way home and feed the kids and all that. Proper little housewife, I was. I used to go with her to cash her cheque once a fortnight, and give her her drinks money. I had to hide the housekeeping or she'd nick it.

You wouldn't believe it now, eh? But if it wasn't for me the whole family would have fallen to pieces.

I didn't mind. It made school hard, that was the only thing. I'd been doing OK at school up till then, but with all the work at home it was hard to keep up. I was up at six most mornings. I'd have done half a day's work before I even left the house. Then as soon as I walked into school they'd be treating me like a kid. Do this, do that, jump to it. You lazy girl, how stupid are you, you can't even do this little bit of homework. I wanted to shout – I could do it, easy, if I wasn't falling asleep at home next to my baby brother after I'd sung him his lullaby. If I hadn't two kids at home to look after, and food to buy and bills to pay and shopping and cooking and washing and Mum to look after as well. But I couldn't say a word. If anyone outside found out about it, it'd be the Social in and that'd be the end of our family.

That's all I wanted. To keep the family together. It's what Mum always said. *We have to keep the family together.*

In the end they found out anyway. One of the neighbours, maybe, or maybe I took too many days off school. If I'd been able to keep school together as well as the housework and all that, maybe our family'd still be together today.

I don't think Mum's ever forgiven me for that.

The Social really did us over. Mum got whisked away to detox. We all got taken into care. Our family was broken to bits. I should have worked harder. I could have worked harder, if I'm honest. I was lazy. Sam and Katie were taken together, but the family that looked after them didn't want me. I was too big, too bloody ugly or something. Too much of a problem.

I still don't get it. One day I was holding everything together for everyone, and the next I'm this problem. How does that happen? For ages I was waiting for it to dawn on everyone that I was the only reason the family kept going, but they never did.

I hadn't seen Mum for nearly a year. Or Katie or Sam. I'd missed their birthdays. I wasn't going to miss Mum's. She was still my mum, wasn't she? She could let me give her a bloody present. She could let me do that much.

They lived in Armly these days, miles away from where we used to be. I was there in twenty minutes. It was so weird. Like they're living on another planet and then you just jump on the bus – and there they are.

I'd got her a really nice present. Mum loves candles.

She used to collect them. Sometimes, she'd light loads of them in the front room when we had a takeaway or something, a couple of dozen or more, and we'd sit around and talk about stuff and eat our food. So I got her some coloured candles in pairs, joined together with their long wicks. When you hung them from your finger, they looked really pretty. I'd saved up for her. And some nice pretty paper to wrap them up in and everything.

When I got there, I lost my nerve and wandered up and down for ages before I finally got it together to go and peer over the wall into the yard. The back door was open; there was someone in. But I still couldn't do it, so I went away and walked around some more, and when I went back there was Katie in the yard, hanging out the washing. I watched her through the crack in the gate for a bit, then I hissed out her name. She came over, and when she saw it was me she slipped out, came to stand with me, out of sight of the house, together in the ginnel, me and her.

She's twelve, Katie – two years older than I was when the Social stepped in. Growing up. Getting her boobs. She was going to have a nice figure, I reckon. She'd grown so much. I thought, *Yeah. It's been months since I've seen any of them.*

'Katie, how are you? It's great to see you,' I said.

'Hello, Billie. What are you doing here?'

'Come to see you, haven't I? It's Mum's birthday, isn't it?'

'Last week, that was.' She glanced back at the house behind her. 'You're late.'

'Ah, give us a break. Is she in?' I asked.

Katie nodded. 'Upstairs.'

'Is she . . . ?' I asked. I meant, drunk.

'No.' Katie pouted and looked at me. 'It's you as drinks now, Billie, not her.'

That was really annoying. She only said that because I came round here when I was drunk once or twice.

'Not like her, not like she used to.'

'She never drinks any more, not now,' said Katie.

'Don't she? That's good, then. I'm glad about that.' And I thought, *Maybe, maybe not. Either way Katie's not going to tell me about it.*

'How's Sam?' I asked.

'He's OK.'

'How's that ear? Are you still getting those infections?'

'Not any more. I haven't had one for years. They said I've grown out of it.'

'Good. That's good, isn't it?'

'I know.'

We stood and looked at each other a while longer.

'You shouldn't be here, Billie,' she said.

'I've got her a present, haven't I? I can give my mum a present, can't I?'

'I know, but you said you wouldn't come.'

'She's my mum and all, you know.'

Katie looked sulky at me. 'It's no good, though, is it, you seeing her,' she said. 'Not for anyone. Not for the family.'

I hated the way she said that – 'the family' – as if I was some kind of enemy from outside – me, who held the whole lot together for all those years.

'Katie, I'm allowed to give my sodding mum a present on her birthday, aren't I?'

She just stood there, didn't say anything.

'Ask her,' I said.

'Billie . . .'

'Just . . . ask her for me, will you?'

Katie scowled at me, but she went inside. I was steaming. Having to ask permission to see your mum. I wasn't surprised, though. I wasn't supposed to be there. I'm not a good thing for the family. Things go wrong when I turn up, apparently.

Katie came back, looking dead sulky.

'It's not a good time,' she said.

'She's pissed, isn't she?'

'No!'

I glared at her. I could help her if she wanted me to, but no. She has to do it all on her own.

I nodded down at the basket full of laundry.

'Doing the washing?' I asked.

'I get my pocket money for it,' said Katie.

I thought, *Yeah, I'll bet*.

Behind her there was a murmur of voices. She glanced over her shoulder into the house and back at me quickly. A man.

I smiled grimly. 'Got a feller, has she?'

'Not really. Just a friend,' she said. She looked at the ground. 'She wouldn't want me telling you,' she said. 'It's none of your business.'

I laughed. I just laughed at her.

'You better go now,' she said.

'I want to see her,' I said.

Katie looked up at me, angry now. 'It's nice to see you, Billie. We all miss you. Mum said thanks for coming to see her. She's talking to the Social about seeing you again when she's . . . when she's better, but she doesn't feel like she can cope right now. It's best you go now. You know? You best go now,' she said. She turned and put her hand on the latch to the gate and waited.

So – sod it, eh? I thought. *Sod this.*

I threw the present down at the ground at her feet and I just went and left her to it. I wasn't about to make life any harder for her than it already was, but I'd been more of a mother to her than that cow in there ever was.

I walked away up the ginnel. I glanced back quick after a few metres, in time to see the curtains on the upstairs window fall. And, yes, I caught a glimpse of her face before she hid it away from me behind the curtains. Then I went away. I sat on the bus and I didn't cry. I made a promise a while ago that she'd never make me cry again, and I've stuck to it. It was hard that day, though.

I don't get it. I looked after us all, and I did it all for her, all for her. So how come, when she came out of detox, when she got herself straight, I was the only one she didn't want back?

Rob

You know what winds me up? What winds me up is when you have a brother so stupid he thinks stamping on snails is clever. And then some poncy grammar-school kid comes along and has a go at him, and you have to defend the little git because he's your brother. Result? Total humiliation. You end up on your arse skidding about in snail juice. And your idiot brother – that's the one you were trying to rescue in the first place – he's laughing at you along with all the rest.

I don't do bullies, but sometimes you can see the attraction. It would be so nice, just once, to hold Davey down in the dirt, sit on his face and fart. A good long wet one. The release of tension . . . bliss.

It looked like it was going to be a good day too. That was the day I made my first friend at Statside. And not just any friend, either. If I told you I'd been rescued by a girl, you'd probably think I was an even bigger wimp than you first thought. But when I tell you that that girl was Billie Trevors, and that she beat up the entire Riley gang to save me, you'd shut your trap. Wouldn't you? You would. If you had any sense you would, anyhow.

I know – it sounds too good to be true. Who would have thought that me, Roly Poly Rob, would be mates with the hardest person in the school? In the world for all I know, because no known human has ever met anyone tougher than Billie Trevors. She's hard, but underneath she's really nice. We have loads in common. We like the same music. We laugh at the same things. We've only had a couple of conversations, but I really think she likes me. She's not like the rest of them here. She doesn't go along with things just because everyone else does. She's the sort of person who'll decide if she likes you or not just on how you get on together.

I wish . . .

This is such a hard school. They're all chavs – it's like the style police. If you're not like them, they think you're some sort of pervert. Kids get beat up for listening to the wrong music or wearing the wrong clothes. Just not being them is, like, an insult. At my old school in Manchester, girls used to like me. Girls like big fellas. But here, if any girl even looked at me, she'd get beat up by the girl chavs for being a pervert! What's that about? Martin Riley had his girlfriend Jess slap me around the other day. He didn't even need to hold me down. I just stood there while she slapped the side of my face until it turned red. Then she spat on my jersey and I had to say, *Thank you, Jess.*

Well, not any more. Billie Trevors is my mate. See Jess slap me now. If that Snailboy had known the kind of people I hang out with, he'd have been on the floor licking up snail juice with his dirty, snaily little tongue. And he'd have been happy to do it too.

Another thing that winds me up is when you miss the bus – because Snailboy got on your bus with his snail friend and you were too slow to hop on after them. And so you have to walk home on your own with snail juice all over your trousers. And then it rains. And you get soaking wet and cold and miserable and you arrive at the front door feeling like a complete idiot because that's what you are.

And there's shouting coming from inside the house.

A lot of it, a lot of life, you can't do much about, but I'd found a great way of coping with the shouting. I didn't even have to think about it any more. I turned up my iPod as high as it goes, so that the awesome sound of Metallica filled me up, top to toe, pouring out of me, like shining beams of light, out of my ears, my mouth and out of my eyes, for all I know. Then I opened the door and walked into the house on a wave of sound.

Metallica solves most problems. You don't have to be angry when Metallica is playing. You don't have to be scared. You don't have to worry. They do all that for you. When I listen to Metallica, I am God.

I waded through the music, past the living room and I arrived at the fridge. The fridge is my friend. You need friends in this world. It wasn't being all that friendly today. I have this dream where I open up the fridge and it's full of cake and Coke and snacks and trifle and chocolate and blocks of cheese. You name it. In the dream I'm thin and that shit Philip is at the bottom of a deep hole. I'm going out with Billie. We're making out *in* the fridge. And Metallica is beamed directly through into my brain.

Bliss.

I took out a big slab of cheese and a pint of milk and I waded on upstairs, through the sea of sound. I got myself settled down at the PC and found myself my favourite heavy-metal site, Dead Friends. Dead friends are the best friends. A skeleton never calls you fat. He never slaps you round the face and makes you say thank you. He is most definitely not a chav. Best of all, he likes the same music I do.

I looked at the pictures and started to rap out the drums on my desk. It felt sooooooo good. That's my dream – to be a proper metalhead in a heavy-metal band playing my heavy-metal drums. It might have come true, once upon a time, when I still had my drums. It was so cool – I was so cool, back in the day. I played every day, every spare moment I had I was on the kit, banging away the pain, drumming in the light. I even had the beginnings of a band with my mate Frankie. I was on drums, he played guitar and sang. It was the coolest thing in my life, playing death metal with Frankie back in the day.

Not any more.

There's a reason why I don't have any drums. That reason is called Philip. He's the stinking pile of dog turds who took my drums away. Philip's done some bad things to me, but that was the worst. I'll never forgive him for that. He didn't just take away my drums – he took away my dreams. No one should ever be allowed to do that to you. Now I have no drums and no dreams – but I still have the music. I'll always have the music.

That'll do for now. It'll have to.

There was a noise far in the distance behind me. I turned round; it was Davey. My heart sank. His mouth was opening and closing. I couldn't hear a thing, but I knew exactly what he was saying.

I jumped up, grabbed him by the shoulders, turned him round and marched him out of the room. He was twisting and pushing but Roly Poly had a grip on him. He was still yelling, but I was yelling and so were Metallica so I couldn't hear a word.

'Out!' I was bawling. 'No! No! Out . . .'

'GGGRRRRRRRRXXXXXXXXOWWWWW,' roared Metallica.

'   ' said Davey. '   , Rob!'

I had him out into the corridor and nearly at his door when he managed to pull one of the earphones out.

In came the world. Screaming and shouting and yelling and tears. Philip and my mum.

'Can we have a game, please, Rob? Can we? Rob, please . . . no, don't, Rob . . .' Blub blub blub, the little shit.

'What can I do? What can I do?' I roared. 'What can I do? What can I do?'

I shoved him away and he went down on his bum in his room. I stuck the earplug back in and ran back to my own room. I turned the sound up and tried to concentrate, but it was ruined. I sat there for a few minutes longer, but it was no good.

I got up and went back down the landing.

He was on his bed, bawling his little eyes out. No, that's not fair. He doesn't do that any more – he's too old. He holds it in better now.

'Come on, then. Game on,' I said.

He didn't look at me, but he turned up in my room a few minutes later. I have Metallica. He has me. That's the way it is.

I got out the Xbox and hooked it up to the TV. Davey sat on the bed. He found my iPod and stuck one of the earphones in.

'You are going to get so battered one day listening to this stuff,' he told me.

He's right. If Martin Riley and the chavpack find out I listen to Metallica, I am dead. For them, listening to metal is one step down from being a nonce.

'No one will ever know,' I told him. I sat down next to him. The screen came on. 'Kill All Enemies,' I said, and we started to play.

Chris

So I get off the bus and I walk home and there's my mum waiting for me in the hall.

'We need a word with you, Chris. In here, please.'

My dad was in the living room with his face set like cement. Wikes had got in touch after all, the sneaky little get.

'Not this again,' I said.

'This again,' said my dad. He whipped out a piece of paper, as if my crimes were too numerous to remember. Maybe they were – for him. 'Let's start at the beginning, shall we?' he said in a tired voice, as if he could hardly be bothered. In fact, of course, he loves it. Exercising power over things that are none of his business is one of his hobbies.

'Getting sent out of lessons. Science.'

'He picks on me.'

'I wonder why?' He glanced at the paper again. 'Rudeness.'

'I'm never rude!' I was offended. I have my principles.

'I always misbehave with the maximum of good manners. It's a rule of mine.'

'You're being rude now,' said my dad.

'That's not being rude – that's being clever. Different thing entirely.'

'Chris, stop it,' said Mum, as my dad bulged with rage, like a mating bullfrog – something that I was going to have to point out to him if this went on much longer.

'Not doing the work is rudeness enough when the teachers are going to the trouble.'

'Of being paid,' I pointed out. I mean, no one's paying me, are they? But I'd said the wrong thing again. I could see it.

'Chris, stop answering back and *listen*,' begged my mum. But Dad was beginning to wind me up. I can be reasonable, why can't he? I sighed and gestured for him to carry on.

There was a pause while they both glared at me.

That was a danger sign, them both glaring. I should have picked up on that. Dad paced a couple of times across the floor while Mum watched him anxiously.

'Homework, not done,' he said, when he had regained control. 'Homework not done *for four years*!' You could see him turning red as he spoke.

'Is it four years now? Wow,' I heard myself saying. I hadn't realized. I was impressed. 'Is that a school record?'

'It's not funny,' bawled my dad. 'You know what's

next, don't you? Exclusion. Is that what you want – to be an excluded boy?'

I sighed again. Quite loudly, I admit. I mean, who's being rude here, him or me? I leave you to judge for yourself. 'I've already told you my views on this one,' I said.

Dad turned purple. I know, I know! I could see it coming. It's my mouth – I can't help it. It just says things. But, be fair, he was asking for it.

'Chris . . .' warned my mum.

'I'm sorry,' I said loftily. 'But I haven't heard anything here today to make me consider changing my position.'

Dad charged. Suddenly he had me by the neck up against the wall, breathing baked beans into my face.

'We've had you tested – there's nothing wrong. We've grounded you, we've stopped your money – that doesn't work. We've had private tutors – that doesn't work. The only thing left is to hit you. And, Chris, I don't want to hit you.'

He dropped me and turned away. There was a long, embarrassed silence.

I brushed myself down. 'If you do that again,' I said, 'I'm going to do it back.' My voice was shaking.

'This is a nice middle-class family,' hissed Mum, glaring at Dad. 'We talk things over. We don't hit one another.'

'I can feel my working-class roots rising to the surface,' muttered my dad.

I'd had enough. 'You can shout all you like – I'm not doing it. It's stupid. You try it. See how you like it.'

'I have tried it,' said my dad. 'I tried it for fourteen years. So did your mother. So has everyone else. Now it's your turn.'

Mum stepped in – the business end, you know?

'Chris. Something has to change. Even the nice teachers, the ones who like you, are fed up. They want to exclude you and send you to the Pupil Referral Unit. It's not a joke. It's *happening*.'

'A son of mine, expelled,' groaned my dad.

'But we've done a deal,' said Mum.

And a mighty crap deal it turned out to be.

I had to stay in every night and do a piece of homework.

'Just one piece,' said my mum encouragingly. 'It's not much.'

'No, not much,' I said. 'So long as you don't count the fact that I've actually spent the whole day at school doing exactly the same thing. The whole day. And the day before that. And the day before that. And the day before that . . . And the day . . .'

'Except when you're not there,' said my dad, and I didn't reply to that, because, if I had, I'd have pointed out I wouldn't be there rather more in future, after this.

In order to make sure I stayed in and did said piece of homework, I was going to be locked in my room. Yes, you heard correctly. Locked in my room, like some sort of terror suspect.

For not doing my homework.

'And one thing you can count on, fella,' said Dad.

'You won't be coming out of there until that piece of work is done.'

'That's, like, prison,' I said. 'I haven't robbed anyone. I haven't mugged anyone. You're being ridiculous. What's the point?'

'The point is the future, Chris,' he snapped.

'The future's tomorrow,' I said. 'I don't want the future tomorrow. I want it NOW.'

'Well, you can't have it,' he sneered, and he closed the door and turned the key, leaving me with – you guessed it. Wikes's frog skin. You know? Last thing in the day you have to do frog skin. Then you go home and you get locked in your room to do more frog skin.

'You just have to meet us halfway,' yelled my mum up the stairs.

You see how far gone these people are? Someone must have changed the rules of maths since she went to school, because, what they taught me, halves means two equal parts, right? But what they mean is I spend one half of my life doing school work at school, then I come home and spend the other half of my life doing school work at home. Halfway? Don't make me laugh.

You might have gathered that this evening was the end result of a long and dreadful power struggle between me and the forces of evil – a struggle that they were bound to lose in the end. I'd lost count of how many meetings me and Mum and Dad have had with various members of staff, experts, counsellors and so on.

At first they thought there must be something

wrong. I had tests. Dyslexia, eyesight, IQ. I must be the most tested person in Leeds. Results – everything is just fine. Then, when they ran out of 'issues', they turned to that old standby, measures. Or, to call it by its proper name, punishments.

What they can't get their heads round is – it's not that I can't do the work. It's that I *disagree* with doing the work.

So I don't do it.

It's not like I'm unwilling to negotiate. I accept that school exists. It's boring, but we have to go. I understand that. I go. I work – so long as they don't take the piss. But when I get home, that's my time. It's called the work/life balance. Look it up. What I do at school, that's their business. What I do at home – that's mine. And I never go to detentions, either. They want to punish me, OK, they have that right – so long as they do it in their own time.

They hate it. It drives them mad. They just cannot understand that I'm acting out of principle. It has to be laziness or stupidity or plain old naughty Chris. The teachers go ape shit about it. My grades, they say. Yeah, right. THEIR grades, they mean. Did you know they get paid on how good their class grades are? They don't get enough A to Cs – down goes their money. I'm hitting them where it hurts – right in the wallet.

Well, sod them. They want me to spend a hundred hours a week helping them crawl up the income pole? No thanks. It isn't even necessary. Even if you are stupid enough to want to go to uni and run up massive debts, why not wait until you're nineteen or twenty? You don't even have to do all these stupid A levels, then. You can do a nice, easy one-year access course and get in almost for free just because you're a grown-up. Why bust a gut doing it the hard way now, when you can do it the easy way just by waiting a few years?

No one, but no one, has given me a sensible answer yet to that one.

I had a look at the work and I knew in about two seconds there was no way I was going to do this stuff. It was so boring I felt faint just looking at it. Boredom is for old people. They like being bored. They have to like it – they lack the energy to enjoy themselves.

I texted Alex. He's one of the lucky ones. He likes work.

I texted, 'Mate! I need some homework.'

Outside my room, the boards creaked. My dad, the warder, on his rounds.

Gently, I got on to a game while I waited for a reply – Nothing House – you know that thing where you have to demolish everything by working out where the weak point is? It's like school or family life in that way. I put it on quiet – I had headphones, but I needed to be on the alert.

I got through two streets and the town museum before Dad was at the door. I could hear the key going round.

'Leave me alone! I'm doing it, aren't I?' I yelled.

'Just checking . . .' The door opening . . . him coming

in. Hurriedly I flicked on the screen back to the frog skin.

'Mum!' I screeched. 'Mum, he's checking up on me! Why can't I be left alone to do it my way?'

We both paused and waited for the response.

'Show him what you've done, Chris. Just do it!' she yelled up. Dad smirked and walked in, snorting like a pig walking into a rubbish tip.

'Give me that.' We had a brief tussle as he pulled the laptop out of my grip and checked my tabs.

'Gaming. I thought so. Right. I'm disconnecting the wireless.'

'You can't do that!'

'Can.'

'But I need online resources . . .'

'You were in the lesson. Just do it.'

Stuffed. I sat and racked my brains for ages, but it was no good. I was going to have to break my principles of four years.

I was going to have to do some homework.

It took hours. Hours and hours. Well, one hour at least – but that's not the point. They had caused me to violate my principles.

Mum let me out. Dad was at the supermarket – she must have sent him away to stop him pestering me.

'Chris, this is wonderful,' she breathed, giving me the full positive-reinforcement job. 'Marvellous! You see how easy it is for you once you get down to it? It could be a little longer perhaps . . .'

'Taken me hours,' I pointed out.

'It's wonderful. Here.' She took out her purse and handed me a fiver. 'And there's more where that came from if you can just keep up this standard of work. OK?'

'Thanks,' I said, dripping with sarcasm. She pretended not to notice. I crammed the fiver in my pocket and ran out of the front door. I was a free man. They'd be playing footie down the rec. I was that happy I almost skipped. As I got close to the rec I broke into a run. I couldn't help it. I thought . . . *I love this, I just love this*. I ran on to the grass and into the game.

I was still angry, though. I'd actually had to do some homework. It had made my brain go all floppy and horrible, working that late in the day.

One thing I was sure of. This. Is not. Ever. Happening. Again.

Billie

I was that upset on the bus I wasn't thinking straight. I didn't work it out till I was nearly home. How come my mum wasn't doing that washing? That's her job. Katie should have been doing her homework or out playing with her mates, not standing in the yard hanging up the washing while Mum stayed in bed drinking with her new bloke.

That's what it's all about. I know. The washing's just the start of it. When she's done that, Katie'll be straight inside doing the hoovering and then getting the dinner on and feeding everyone and then washing up, then getting Sammy off to bed. Mum feeling tired, was she? I bet she was. I bet she was feeling so tired she had to lie in bed upstairs with some bloke getting pissed while my little sister ran the whole house for her. The whole mess starting again. Katie not getting her homework done. Katie getting into trouble at school. Mucking up her whole life trying to solve Mum's problems for her.

No way was I going to let our Katie end up like me.

I nearly went straight back to sort it out there and

then. That bloke was there, but I wasn't scared of him. There was no point going down the Social. I tried that before. You know what they said? Told me to stay away. Can you get that? My own family, and now suddenly it's none of my business because that drunken cow wants to get pissed in peace? And no one is there for you, and no one, no one, no one is willing to help you sort it out. Even Hannah.

'You have to leave it to the Social now, Billie,' she said. She said that to me, and she knows exactly how crap they are.

No way. Even if I have to go down for it. I'm going down anyway, for something – everyone knows that. She's ruined my life, but Katie doesn't have to end up like me, does she? Not if I have a say in it.

I was too upset to deal with it right then. I didn't know what to do with myself. I didn't want to go home to Barbara and Dan. I tried ringing Hannah, but she never picks up at this time of day. It's her time with her kid.

Cookie'd be in work . . . Nah. I really wasn't in the mood for that. There was nothing for it. I had to go home.

I was praying, just praying they hadn't found out about that fight in the car park. I could have done with a break right then. But I should have known. I opened the front door and there he was, Dan, waiting for me. She always pushes him out first to do the dirty work.

'What?'

'We . . . we need to see you, Billie. In here. Please?' he added, trying to be nice.

We went through. There she was, Queen Barbara, sitting in her armchair psyching herself up.

'Here we are again, then,' she sniffed.

'What?'

'Fighting, Billie,' said Dan. 'You agreed. No more fights.'

I knew it! 'Who says?' I demanded.

'Mrs Greene saw you from the bus,' said Dan. He pulled a face – like, ouch.

Barbara glared at him. 'United front, Daniel,' she pointed out. See? A bit of human kindness – no chance.

'It's not like that,' I said. 'You can't just stop – everyone wants a pop. You have to work at it. I'm doing my best.'

'It's not enough,' said Barbara.

'But I'm getting there,' I begged. 'I've been trying really hard – doesn't that count for anything? I'm really, really doing my best . . .'

It was no use. She just sat there with her lips pressed together like two slices of cold ham.

Dan let out a breath. 'You've been on your last chance, Billie.'

'I've really tried. I've been on a fight diet. Just one a week,' I said, trying for a bit of fun.

Barbara doesn't do fun. 'You promised,' she hissed. 'You promised, Billie. How many times have you promised?'

'I know, I know.' I looked at Dan. I felt like one of

those puppies you see in the ads – the ones with the begging eyes. I was thinking, *Don't throw me out, don't make me go back into care, don't make it so I mucked this one up as well – please please please . . .*

They both sat there and let me hang.

Barbara and Dan are the fifth foster carers I've had. So far. People always get rid of me. Have you noticed that? They always dump you in the end. It's just a question of when. But me, I'm so stupid, every single time I imagine it's going to be different.

'You're grounded,' she announced finally.

'Oh, thank you, Barbara, thanks, I'm really sorry, I won't let you down again.'

She nodded, and pulled a face. 'One month,' she said.

'What?' A month? That's unheard of. No one can stay in for a month. 'You can't –'

'You can't be trusted outside. No, Billie. One last, final chance. The absolute last time, Billie. I promise you that. One month.'

'Just accept it, Billie,' said Dan. 'You've had it coming, love,' he added.

'But a month . . .' I'd had enough. 'It's stupid – it's just a set-up. We all know I won't manage a month. You just want to get rid of me . . .'

I could feel tears coming. I headed for the door, but Dan was in the way.

'You stay there, Daniel,' ordered Barbara, before he could move. And poor guy, all he wanted to do was get out the way, but he did as he was told and stood there and quivered. I did once, see. A couple of times. I've lost it with him before. It's not his fault.

'It's all right,' I said quietly. 'I'm not going to hit you.'

And then, for no reason, for no reason at all, Barbara went ape shit.

'Don't you dare threaten us,' she snarled.

'What are you on?' I said.

'Gently, Billie . . .' said Dan.

But I was really running out of patience. 'She's looking for it, though, isn't she?' I said.

'She's scared of you, Billie,' he said. 'We both are.'

Barbara went bonkers. She jumped up out of her chair, snapping away like a nasty little dog. 'I'm not scared of her! She might bully her friends, but she isn't going to bully me,' she yelled.

'Don't start at me like that, Mrs,' I told her. 'I'll knock you down, no problem. I'm only laying off because I know what it's like living with a dried-up old bitch like you . . .'

I couldn't help it! I watched the words coming out of my mouth and then before she could answer I ran off. I knew, if she went on, I was going to blow. I pushed Dan out of the way and ran upstairs into my room. And her, silly cow, you know what she does? I mean, she's won, hasn't she? All she has to do is leave me to cry it out, but no. She runs after me to the foot of the stairs and yells up at me . . .

'No wonder your mother never wanted you back. Who bloody would?'

*

I wish I could go deaf. You can't help hearing things. She knows I can't cope with that. That's why she said it.

I went. The red mist. I've done loads of work with Hannah about it, but it never does any good, not when people are going on about me mum. I waved my hand and tried to clear the air, but the red mist came down anyway and the next thing I knew . . .

I don't know how long it took – not long probably. Minutes. It's amazing the mess you can make in just a few minutes. When I came round, I sat down on the bed and I just cried.

The shelves were down. The curtains were down; the curtain rail was on the floor. The mirror was smashed; the desk was kicked over. And I'm, like, *No no no no no! Please no!* What is it with me? Just looking at it made me want to wreck the place all over again.

Jesus. What was going to happen to me now?

I sat there for a while. Then I did what Hannah taught me to do. I took three long breaths, got up and started to tidy up. This was going to be a bloody big deal. They had me in respite care for a week last time. I'd been on my last legs ever since.

But you know what? It was a relief, really. I been trying and trying and trying, but it was so, so hard. I felt, like, *There you go, that's it, then*. Billie's a lunatic – she's not fit for a proper life. We always knew it. Take her away. At least now we don't have to waste any more of our time trying to turn her round.

There was a huge long shard of glass from the mirror lying on the floor shaped like a cutlass, so I picked that up in one of the curtains to save my hand – and it was then, of course, that Barbara came charging up the stairs and burst in. I thought she was going to hit me so I lifted my hand in the air to hold her off . . .

'Ahhhhhhhhhhhhh! Oh my God! Dan, help! She's going to kill me!'

Off she went, down the stairs like I was about to chop her head off. I thought, *What now?* Then I caught sight of myself in what was left of the mirror – standing there with this huge blade of glass raised up over my head, my face half red and half white, my eyes glaring and pulling a face like a madwoman. No wonder! I'd have laughed if it wasn't so awful.

I ran to the door. 'I'm not going to hurt you! Barbara? I'm not going to hurt you! OK?'

She was out in the street by then. I don't know if she heard me or not. 'Dan, Dan! Call the police!' she was screaming. 'She's gone psycho, she's gone psycho!'

It really was not my day.

I was halfway through sorting the room out when I heard the sirens. I thought, *She hasn't. It must be for someone else.* Down the main road they came . . . up John Street, nearer and nearer. Up our road.

She bloody had.

I was still hoping when the cars screeched to a halt outside the front door and the doors started slamming. It was like something on the telly. I went to the window to have a look. Three cars – three! – and a van. The van doors burst open and there was a flurry of cops diving for cover. They move fast, those boys, I'll say that. I peered down. What were they up to?

Leaning over the car there was this cop with a rifle trained on me.

A rifle?

I couldn't believe it. The armed-response unit? Was this really happening? There was even a little dot of red bobbing around my chest.

'Put your weapon down and come out with your hands up,' someone said – some big chief hiding in the shrubbery or something.

'You what?'

'Put your weapon down and come out with your hands up,' he repeated.

'What weapon, you morons? I'm fifteen – oh, forget it . . .'

I didn't even bother. I just went back into the room and got on with the clearing up. Outside I could hear Barbara yelling at them.

'Don't put that gun down! She's gone psychotic. You don't know what she's going to do next.'

Even after that they didn't dare come into my room. I shouted, 'Knock and enter,' when I heard them on the stairs, but they insisted on hiding round the corner. They even tried to get me to come out backwards on my hands and knees. No way. I walked out head first, like I always do.

'I've got me catapult with me, you better watch it,' I told them, and they all smiled like girls and stood around in their body armour, and their weapons quivering in the air, not knowing what to do with themselves.

Pathetic.

They were *furious*. God only knows what she'd told them – they must have thought I had an AK47 in there or something. They got me downstairs and she was waiting there to watch it, her and Dan. She was crying her eyes out, like it was her that was going away to get locked up.

'I'm sorry, Billie, I'm sorry, I'm sorry,' she kept saying.

The big chief was telling her off while I was bent over the car getting searched.

'This isn't the kind of matter we normally use an armed-response unit for, Mrs Barking,' he said.

'I'm so sorry,' she whispered. 'I think I might have panicked a little bit.'

The copper sighed. 'Billie's going to get put away sooner or later, Mrs Barking. It's just a matter of time. But, until she does, we have enough real criminals to deal with. You could be arrested yourself for wasting police time, you do realize that?'

The cops eased me into the back seat while she stuck her nose into Dan's shoulder and wailed. I looked round as we drove off. He actually had the nerve to wave me goodbye.

Chris

It was getting dark at the rec. People were starting to drift away.

I had a plan. Like all works of genius, it was blindingly obvious once you knew it, yet almost impossible to guess until you did. It couldn't fail. It was too simple to fail.

I don't go home.

It's perfect! Obvious, yet unexpected. Lock me in my room when I'm not there – how do you do that? Make me do homework while I'm out playing footie with the lads – I don't think so. Devastating.

Of course there were one or two technical details to work out, like eating, drinking, having a few quid in my pocket, somewhere to sleep. Those kinds of things are easy enough to organize, though. I raid our fridge when Mum and Dad are out at work. I stay with my mates; their parents feed me. Problem solved.

Despite the likes of Wikes going on about me being rude, I am actually very polite when I want to be – polite enough for people's mums to take a shine to me.

It isn't hard. All you have to do is give them a big smile whenever you see them and tell them how wonderful their cooking is and what a warm cosy home they have, and they're just about ready to adopt you.

'All right if I stay at your place tonight?' I asked Alex – not going into too much detail. Alex takes fright too easily.

He looked down and shuffled his feet. 'Don't think you'll be able to,' he said.

'Why not?'

'Mum . . .'

'She won't mind,' I told him. She's never said no yet.

'Yeah, but your dad rang up.'

'What?'

'He told her you weren't to stay.'

'He never!'

'Yeah.'

The bastard was on a mission. I looked around for someone else. 'Mickey . . .'

'Sorry, mate. He rang mine up as well.'

'How can he ring yours up? He doesn't have your number.'

Mickey scratched his eyebrow and looked over at Alex.

'What's going on?' I asked.

'Mum wanted the land lines,' muttered Alex.

'And you told her?'

'I didn't have any choice – she asked me!'

'You just say no, Alex!'

'She put pressure on me,' wailed Alex, the loathsome

worm. 'She said it was for your own good because you were falling behind at school.'

'Jesus, Alex, you pile of fluff. That's me stuffed, isn't it?'

A quick roll-call revealed that it was all true. Alex, my so-called best friend, had handed over the entire contents of his address book to my dad, who'd spent the rest of the evening on the phone telling everyone that I needed rescuing from myself. Can you believe that?

'Alex, this is new heights of cowardice even for you.'

'Gotta go,' whined Alex. 'Said I wouldn't be late. See you.' He ran off.

'Sorry, mate,' said Mickey.

'Can't I sleep on your floor anyway?' I asked. 'Sneak me in.'

'Not really, mate. Sorry.'

One by one they all deserted me. I was on my own.

Back at home, Dad was being smug. Thought he had it cracked, didn't he? So me, I was smug right back. I looked at him and smiled a smile that said, 'You think you've got me? You're so far from getting me you're not on the right motorway. You're not even in the right country, you grey, balding control freak.'

That took the 's' right out of his smug and you know what that made him, don't you? You could see it in his face, draining away, all the 's', trickling down his chin and making his T-shirt all wet and sticky down the front. He tried to keep it up for a bit, but I couldn't help myself and turned up the smug all the way to full frontal cheese. That's when he started shouting.

'He's up to something,' he said. 'Doreen, look at him – look at the way he's *smiling*!'

I dropped the smug – too late.

'It's no good, Chris. I've been watching you. Stop winding your father up. He's only doing this for your own good – you know that perfectly well.'

I gave her my best complacent shrug. She paused.

'There's nothing he can do, nowhere he can go,' she said to Dad. 'We've rung up all his friends; he has no money. He's just putting on a brave front. This time, we've got him.'

But you could hear the doubt in her voice even as she spoke.

Rob

It was a bad one. It went on for hours. Me and Davey stayed upstairs out of the way with the Xbox on loud. Whenever Mum or Philip came up to use the loo, we turned the sound down so they wouldn't come in to moan at us.

How rubbish am I? If I was worth anything, I'd be down there as soon as he raised his voice to her. I'm a big lad – big as Philip, I reckon. But I never do. You know why? Because I'm too scared. I'm a coward. I sit up here instead, playing computer games and pretending nothing's happening.

Billie wouldn't do that. If someone was speaking to her mum like that, she'd be straight down there. *Bam bang whack!* You should see her. She's that fast you can't even see what she does. And down they go. I could never tell her. If she knew what a wimp I really am, she'd never speak to me again. She's the Queen of Pain. Me, I am the shit in fear's pants.

I didn't use to be like this.

'Go, just go, go go go!' screams Mum downstairs.

'It's my house! Why should I leave my own house, you silly cow?' he screams back.

It's Philip. He turned me into shit. He turned my mum into shit. He turns everything into shit. Davey's staring hard at the Xbox trying to ignore the noise, and I'm thinking, *It's all right for you – he likes you.*

Davey's his son. Me, I'm just the fat lump that gets in his way.

Hours they were at it. How can you find so much to argue about? We were starving hungry. In the end I sneaked out and got us some chips – I didn't have enough for fish. But chips were OK.

It quietened down sometime after ten. He went out. I went to bed. I'd had enough. We'd been playing Xbox for hours. Davey wanted to go on – he can go on all night – but I'd had it. As soon as Philip left, I sent Davey out and got into bed and just lay there. I wanted to get up and see if Mum was OK, but I thought, *I'll let her get herself together first. She won't want me to see her just yet.* I heard Davey creeping downstairs. I thought, *I'll just close my eyes for a minute and then I'll go down too . . .*

I must have fallen asleep because the next thing I knew, Mum was sitting on the side of my bed, going, 'Robbie, love, you awake, love?'

I sat up, all dopey, and started remembering.

'You all right?' I asked her.

'Well, you know,' she said.

'That was a big row,' I told her. 'Davey was right scared.'

'I know, love. You did really well by him. He told me about it, playing up here with him all evening. Buying him chips.' She smiled sadly and stroked my hand. 'I'm not very good at being a mum, am I?'

It really annoys me when she speaks like that. 'You're a great mum. It's not you.' There was a pause. We looked at each other. 'Where's Philip?' I asked – kind of hoping he'd somehow gone and left us to it.

'Out,' she said. 'Hey, love, look, I've got something for you.'

She handed me over this carrier bag. A present. It wasn't even my birthday. I reached inside and hoiked out . . . Guess what? Only a Metallica T-shirt. No – only *the* Metallica T-shirt. I could hardly believe it. I turned it over to read the back to see if it said what I was hoping it said.

It did.

'Oh, man! It's awesome. Mum, just look at it. Oh, you beauty!'

'D'ya like it?'

Like it? It was the best thing I'd ever owned. On the front was this evil skeleton on a bike and on the back in letters of blood it said . . .

CRACK-SMOKING
FUDGE-PACKING
SATAN-WORSHIPPING
MOTHERFUCKER

It was sooo beautiful I wanted to cry. I just flung my arms round her and gave her a great big roly poly love.

'Ah, Mum, where'd you get the money?' I asked, suddenly thinking how skint she was.

'Been saving for you.'

'What did I do to deserve this?' I jumped out of bed in my pants. I didn't care – I wouldn't have cared if I was naked. I pulled on the T-shirt so I could see in the mirror.

'Look at that! Look at me! Do I look good or what?'

'You're terrific, love. You look great.'

'I do, don't I? I look great.'

'You deserve it, Robbie. The way you look after Davey. You deserve everything anyone can ever give.'

I was still turning round in the mirror, looking at myself.

'I know things aren't good at the moment,' said Mum. 'Davey needs you, though, Robbie. You won't forget that, will you?'

'Don't you worry. I'd look after a house full of Daveys for this. You're in credit, Mum.'

I got back into bed and we had another big love, then she got up to go. I snuggled down. She looked at me and laughed. 'You're not sleeping in it, are you?'

'Sleeping in it? I'm living in it!'

'You won't go to school in it, though?'

'Don't worry. I'll keep it under my jumper. No one'll know.'

She was right, though. Wearing a shirt with fudge-packer and that written on the back of it to my school – suicide. But no way was I taking it off. I'd just have to be dead careful, that's all. Or dead. One or the other. Just then I didn't even care.

See why I love my mum? She's got no money, she has such a hard life, and still finds the time to save up and get me this. A shirt like this, let me tell you – they don't come cheap.

'I love you, Mum.'

She bent down and kissed me. I curled my toes. I felt about five years old. It was great.

'Don't forget – look after Davey, won't you?'

'Don't worry. I'm here for him.'

'I know you are, love. Night!'

'Night, then.'

She left. I went to sleep thinking, *I'm the luckiest guy in the world. Drums, who needs them?*

That was the best night of my life so far. If it never got any better than that, I'd die well happy.

Billie

They take your shoelaces and belt off you before they lock you up so you can't hang yourself. It's this welded box. No windows. The door's as thick as your leg. Solid steel. When it closes, it's like the rest of the world just disappears. You can scream and howl and bang – it makes no difference. All you can do is sit there and try not to go mad.

Barbara – what a cow! Going on about my mum – she knows I can't bear it. It's her way of dumping me. Then she can say, *See – it wasn't my fault. Billie blew it again.*

And then calling the cops on me. The armed-response unit. So that'll be on my record now. Thanks, Barbara. Just what I needed. They had me fooled for a while. Barbara and Dan, and Hannah and Jim at the Brant. Just for a bit I thought I might actually get my head sorted out, get myself some kind of a life. But it's like a game they play. It keeps them in work.

I bet they'll charge me with assault, even though I

never laid a hand on her. It won't even be the WASP now – it'll be the Secure Unit. Prison for kids. And if that happens, they can take my belt and my shoelaces away all they like, but I won't live like that. I'll find a way somehow, even if I have to bite my own veins open, I swear it.

Get it over with, Billie. Just stop mucking around and just . . . get it done.

I don't know how long they left me there. Hours. They had that bastard Farrell on the desk when I came in – he's only in the job because he can bully people. I knew when he came off shift because the nice one came in with a cup of tea. Jolly. He's the most miserable-looking copper you ever saw in your life, but once you get to know him he's not so bad. For a copper. The first time I saw him he came into the cell with a cup of tea and stood there looking like his mum had just died or something.

'They call me Jolly. You can see why.'

'No, I can't see why,' I told him – pretty fed up at the time.

'It's my name,' he said. 'Jolly.'

I didn't get it at the time. It made me laugh later on, though. This time he came in with my shoes and stuff and sat on the bench next to me.

'Armed assault this time, Billie. You're moving up fast,' he said.

'They're never getting me for armed assault! I never touched anyone.'

Jolly sat there and watched me for a bit. 'Well, you got away with it again,' he said at last. 'There's no charges. You're still on a lucky streak.'

'Lucky? And me in here? You must be joking.'

'Pretty lucky, if you ask me,' he said. 'Waving half-metre shards of glass in people's faces. She could have had you for threatening behaviour if nothing else.'

I was bent down doing up my laces. I looked sideways up at him. 'Armed-response unit,' I said.

He just looked back.

'Armed-response unit,' I repeated.

'She must have been scared silly,' he pointed out. I waited. Finally, Jolly raised his eyebrows. 'Not going to look good on report, is it?' he said. He leaned in closer. 'The chief spent fifteen minutes in there giving them a right roasting. I saw them in the canteen after. Pretty fed up they looked, especially when one of the lads asked if he could have an armed guard to get him down to the sweet shop and back.'

I started sniggering, but he didn't crack a smile. He never does.

'Think it's funny, do you?' he said. 'You won't when you meet any of that lot out there.' He jerked his head to the outside. 'And I thought your name was mud already.'

Very bloody Jolly. But it was true. The coppers hate me already. Now I'd made fools of the armed response. It's not fair! It wasn't me made fools of them – it was her, that Barbara.

Not that they need any help.

Jolly nodded and stood up. 'Your social worker's here.'

'Where am I going?' I asked, following him out of the cells. Jolly shrugged.

In the corridor we passed one of the coppers who'd been at the house on the way out. I couldn't resist it.

'What, you still here, not out terrorizing toddlers today, then?' I asked him. 'I heard someone had his sweets nicked round the corner. You could always go and blow him away.'

'Well done, Billie, that'll make you popular,' said Jolly quietly.

'Do you blame me?'

He didn't answer. I took that for a no.

My social worker, Jodie Grear, was waiting out front. I was putting it on, strutting it up for the sake of the coppers, but once we were outside and she was opening her car for me to get in, reality hit home.

'What's going to happen to me?' I asked her.

'You're in luck, Billie. I managed to get respite for you, for a few nights anyway.'

I got in the car. It was supposed to be good news. I suppose it was. I could have ended up in the cells overnight. But you know what? I think I might have preferred that to another carer. Five of 'em in four years. It does my head in. I'm thinking, *Are they going to be hard bastards? Are they going to feed me well? Are they going to be nice? Do they want me to be part of the family, or just another client?*

At least in the cells no one wants to be your mum.

Jodie started up the car and pulled away, chatting about stuff. Trying to make things feel normal, I suppose. That's what they do. As if picking me up from the nick and trying to find me a bed for the night is normal.

'Sorry,' I said suddenly.

'What for?' she asked.

'Hauling you out. You should be at home watching telly.'

'Oh, don't worry, love. It's what I'm paid for.'

Yeah, I thought. *It's what you're paid for.* Jodie rattled on, but I had to turn my face away. People have to be paid to bother with me. I ought to be nationalized, me. I'm a whole bloody industry, all on my own.

We pulled up outside a terrace house. I had no idea which road it was on. I sat there staring at the door. Big old Billie, that's me. But when you're there staring at yet another front door and wondering what's behind it, you feel about two years old.

Rob

I got up, got dressed, no socks. I had 'em last night. Where do they go, socks? So I tiptoed down the corridor and tapped on their door. Mam always knows where there's socks. I opened the door. Philip's lying there, Mam's a lump under the covers.

I cleared my throat. The lump moves and a face pokes out. Never seen her before.

I closed the door. Jesus Jesus Jesus. Where's my mum?

I went downstairs. I got the cereal out. It was getting late. I was thinking I ought to get Davey up. I was scared. There was a movement upstairs – someone going to the loo. Him. I froze. The footsteps stopped. I sat down to eat my cereal and then they started up again. Along the landing. Down the stairs. It's him. He came all the way down and stood behind me, but he still made me jump when he spoke.

'Robbie.'

I jumped so hard I spilt the cereal down me front – down THE T-shirt! I started frantically mopping it up.

'What is that?' he said, staring at the T-shirt.

'Metallica,' I said. 'Mum gave it me.'

'Did she now?' He pulled a face. 'Well, don't go wearing it to school. You'll get battered.' He nodded upstairs. 'Two teas, there's a good lad.' I looked up. He winked.

'Yeah, yeah, no problem,' I said.

He turned to go. Upstairs, I could hear Davey moving about.

'Philip?'

He turned his head.

'Where's me mam?'

He shrugged slightly. 'She's left us, Robbie.'

'Where to?'

'I dunno. Her sister in Manchester, I suppose.' He turned round to watch my reaction. 'It's just us now, eh, son?' he said.

I wasn't his son. And yeah. It was just us now.

Davey came down. Philip put his arm round him. 'Dat's ma boy,' he said. That's what he says all the time.

Davey yawned and he turned round to look at me and he saw the T-shirt. His eyes almost jumped out of his head.

'You're not going to wear that to school, are you? Dad! Don't let him wear that to school. He'll get battered.'

'That's his lookout, isn't it?'

'But, Dad . . .'

'Two teas – quick, like, eh, Robbie?' said Philip.

I looked up at him and in that moment, while Davey

was looking at me and not at him, he put his finger to his lips, nodded his head at Davey and winked again. Then he turned and left us to it.

It wasn't fair, that, making me keep his dirty little secrets for him, like it was me and him in it together. Like I was his mate. If I was Billie, I'd have whacked him right there and then. Davey was going to find out – he was bound to. He had a right to know that his mum had gone and his dad was upstairs in bed with another woman. But I wasn't going to tell him, because I always do what Philip tells me, every time.

I can see it in his eyes when he looks at me. 'You're shit,' his eyes say. 'I made you shit and I'm going to keep you shit, and there's nothing you can do about it.'

He's right. I am shit. I can never forgive him for doing that to me. And I can never forgive myself for letting him. So instead of just telling Davey anyway, I went round the house looking for a note. I wanted her to tell him, see. There was a note last time she left. I went round and round the house looking for it, but of course I never found one because if there ever was one, Philip had already taken it away.

But I knew what was going on, really. There was a note. The T-shirt was the note. The visit last night was the note. The time she'd spent with Davey before she came in to see me was the note. She wanted our good-byes to be nice and if she'd told us face to face then it would have been horrible. But I wish she had told us, because now it was all on my plate – what to do about Davey and everything. And I hadn't got a clue.

There was only one good thing in my life that day. Yeah – you got it. The T-shirt. That was all I had left of my mum. It was her goodbye and her thanks, and her way of saying she loved me, and her see you later. I was wearing it under my school jumper, next to my skin and that's where it was going to stay. In my mind, I'd already decided it was never coming off, ever. Until I saw her again, anyhow.

I told Davey I'd left it at home to keep him happy. It was all right – no one could see. We're at the bus stop. Kids gathering. The bus to Reedon High comes sailing past. I'm not taking any notice. I'm not even thinking. I'm trying to feel T-shirt and Metallica and good . . .

And then this splash comes out of nowhere. Big splash, right down my front. I pull my jumper out – and it's only Ribena. I could smell it. Blackcurrant all over my school jumper. Which meant . . .

'Who did that!' I screamed. 'Who did that?'

'Someone on the bus – I saw it coming down,' yelled Davey. 'I think they spat,' he added.

'I'll kill them,' I roared. 'I'll bloody mash them!' Because it was soaking right through . . . yeah! Right underneath to the sacred T-shirt. No way was I going to let Ribena get on my Metallica T-shirt. Blood, maybe. Piss, shit, bring it on. But Ribena and Metallica?

Never.

I hoiked off my school jumper. There was a big stain right on the pale patch next to the skeleton's legs.

'Who did that? I'll kill them!' I howled. I wasn't thinking I was that mad.

Davey's eyes practically fell out of his head when he saw what I had on. 'What are you doing?' he hissed. 'You can't wear that! It's asking for it. Put it on – people'll see.'

I'd had enough. I'd been bathed in snail juice, humiliated and left by the only person who really loves me. The T-shirt was all I had. I pulled it out and stuck it in his face. 'I don't care any more, Davey. This is ME,' I told him. 'See? This. Is. Me!'

But Davey wasn't looking. He was staring up the road behind me. 'Here comes Riley,' he whined. 'Put it on, put it on, quick.'

I put it on quick enough then. No point in getting battered for nowt. And I was quick too – I move fast for a big lad. I got the jumper on in loads of time and stood there looking all innocent while Martin Riley, the King of the Chavs, and his little bunch of mini-chavs came up behind me. No one would have guessed that under that school jumper I had a detailed description of everything they hated most written all over my back.

Except that I'd not pulled the jumper down far enough. It was up at the back. While I was standing there feeling safe and right, Riley and his chavpack was reading – they could just about read – the word 'Motherfucker' writ right across my arse. The first I knew of it was him pulling up my jumper.

'Gerroff!' I yelled.

Riley read the rest of the message. His eyes bulged; his face turned puce. 'You pervert,' he barked.

'I can explain,' I said.

Then him and his mates closed in and I hit the deck.

Chris

Tuesday morning. Breakfast. My parents – or should I call them my jailers – ate their morning toast *suspiciously*. Mum's quite good at hiding how she feels but Dad just can't help himself. He kept casting me angry little glances as if he didn't trust me. Mum was being . . . not smug, she doesn't do smug. She does confident. It amounts to the same thing. It's the same as smug, only better concealed.

In this respect, oddly, my stupid dad is better than my clever mum. It's not intelligence. It's instinct. She'd thought it through and decided that nothing could go wrong; their plans were watertight. But my dad knew instinctively that somehow I was going to find a way round it.

He was right.

I sneaked back home at lunchtime to get the stuff I needed for Plan B. I had hoped to have Alex with me, despite the fact that he'd proved himself about as trustworthy as a sack of scorpions. One last chance.

'But I don't want one last chance,' he whined. I gave it to him anyway, but then we fell out on the way to school. I did a Bad Thing on the bus. We were sitting together as usual. I was swigging blackcurrant juice out of one of those squirty bottles when we went sailing past the stop where the Statside kids were waiting – and guess who was there? None other than Roly Poly, the snail cruncher, standing there with his evil little brother.

I didn't even have to think about it. I stuck the bottle out of the window and gave it a good hard squeeze. A long snake of purple juice wiggled its way down and – bingo! – splash! Right on the fat one's front.

The results were spectacular. He started dancing about on the pavement, bending over almost double in his efforts to pull the jumper off over his head. It was bizarre. You'd have thought it was sulphuric acid or something, not a humble fruit drink. Then he actually dashed out into the road after the bus, as if he was going to catch it and tear it to pieces with his bare hands.

Wow.

As soon as we were out of sight, Alex turned on me. 'You shouldn't have done that. He's going to kill you now, if he finds out that was you. Oh, mate! You're on your own with this one,' he said, sitting back and crossing his arms.

'I always am on my own when you're around, Alex,' I told him. The hypocrite – he'd been laughing his face off just moments before. But he was right. I shouldn't have done it. I wasn't expecting Roly to go actually mad. What sort of monster is it that loves his T-shirt so much he's prepared to try and beat up a bus for it?

'Why do you always have to get into trouble?' he said. 'Why can't you just be more like everybody else?'

I rolled my eyes. 'Why would anyone want to be like everybody else?' I asked him.

'Because that's how you get on. Because it's how the world works,' he told me.

By the time we got to school, we were both steaming. I didn't even bother reminding him he'd said he'd help me out at lunchtime.

I run the business from the garage. There's an old PC where I keep my database and go online. The Wi-Fi doesn't get to the garage so I have to run a cable through to the router. The business goes in phases; it was in a quiet phase just now because Mum and Dad had frozen my assets. That was the last attempt to make me knuckle down. Freezing my assets – like I was Colonel Gaddafi or something. The lengths these people go to is unbelievable. I'll get sent to Guantanamo Bay at this rate.

I had some good stuff there waiting to be sold on. Vintage clothes are a big thing. The older the better. You turn them from jumble into vintage by sending them to the cleaners and putting a label on them saying 50s DRESS, or 70s RETRO, or even 80s if it's really crap. I bought most of it from charity shops and jumble sales, but some of it was liberated from Mum and Dad's wardrobe and drawers. Mum in particular has some sort of shoe and dress fetish. She never wears most of them. Other people do. I call them customers.

They freeze my assets, I liberate theirs. Who started it? That's all I ask.

There's some other bits and pieces. Some of my stuff I hadn't got round to flogging yet. My old Scalextric. My bike – it's a good one. I try not to use it much in case I scratch it and affect the resale value. Dad's bass guitar's down there too. That isn't mine, but it will be one day. The way I see it, they're going to leave it all to me in their wills anyway, so it's just, you know, getting a preview.

There's my old drum kit too. I got it a couple of years ago. Christmas present. I fancied the idea of being in a rock 'n' roll band, pulling loads of girls and getting off my face all night, but once I actually had the drums I realized – that's not the same thing as sitting for hours on end practising hitting things with sticks.

The gear I wanted today was hidden behind a heap of plywood. Camping gear. There was a reasonable-sized four-man tent and a two-man that I bought off eBay to resell. It was a bargain. There was also a gas camping stove, plastic mugs and stuff like that from when we used to go on camping holidays years ago. No one had used any of it for years.

I took the four-man. The two-man was lighter, but it might end up a longish holiday.

That was about it. Oh – money. Yeah, I had to take that out of the food kitty. They don't usually notice if you just get a few quid. This was different – I took forty, which was fair – they put in a hundred a week and it takes more to feed one.

I had it all worked out. You'd never guess. I was going to camp out – actually on the school grounds. Genius, eh? No one was ever going to think of looking for me there. Our school has acres and acres of land. A load of it is footie and rugby pitches, most of which never get used. It all dissolves round the edges where there's a river and it turns into woodland and bushes and stuff. I'd found a great spot, hidden away among some bushes.

It was perfect. I'd go to school, hang around with my mates in the evening, kip in the tent overnight – and that's me. Just until the heat dies down, you know?

Round two to Mum and Dad. They had made me do homework for the first time in four years. But was I broken? Was I giving in? I don't think so.

Round three to moi.

Rob

It wasn't the beating. A kid like me gets beatings. It was the T-shirt. What they'd done to that.

They'd spat on it; they'd rolled it in the mud. They'd stamped it into the puddles and the shit and the grass. One minute it was perfect – the next, it was a hopeless mess.

At least I still had it on. They'd done everything they could to get it off me but I hadn't let go. The harder they kicked, the harder I curled up round it. I hadn't bothered protecting myself. I didn't matter – it was the T-shirt that mattered. I just curled up and clung on while they kicked and spat and ripped at it.

I went straight to the toilets when I got to school. I could have cried. I did cry, as it happens.

It was trashed. Filthy. Someone had tried to rip the skeleton off the front and the wheel of his bike was flapping about. I'd only had it a few hours and it was ruined. Why do people always go for the things you care about? Why do they want to hurt you where it hurts the most?

And it was then, at the lowest moment of my life, that the miracle happened.

If you'd have been standing there, you'd never have known. It wasn't the kind of miracle where something unbelievable happens while you're stood there watching, like the lame walking or that sort of thing. It was inside. I suddenly realized . . .

Me mam's left me to be looked after by a man who hates my guts – the man who stole my dreams off me when I was small and who turns me into shit every day. I've got no friends. I've been rolled in the mud, I've been spat on, I've been abused, I've been treated like dirt, and my T-shirt, which was about the only good thing in my life, has been torn, muddied and spat on. But you know what? All they've done is make it better! Because this is no ordinary T-shirt. This is a *heavy-metal T-shirt*. This is Metallica. This T-shirt doesn't want to be nice and new and clean. It *wants* to be torn. It *wants* to be covered in blood and sweat and tears and snot. It wants to be rolled in the shit. This T-shirt, it needs to be ripped about and nearly torn off your back before it's even born.

See what I mean? All they'd done, Riley and his gang of chavs – they'd christened my T-shirt. They'd made it better. They'd made it *real*.

Isn't it amazing how just thinking something can change your whole life? That's what a miracle is. Not flashing lights and choirs of angels and people coming back to life. It can happen in a moment and no one would ever know but the person it's happening to. It was like that.

For the first time in my life, I wasn't just a fan – I was living the dream. I *was* metal. Suddenly, from being the worst day in my life, it was the best. I had this crazy feeling; things were never going to get better than this.

'Thank you!' I shouted. 'Thank you for beating me up. Thank you for rolling me in the dirt! Thank you, thank you. You made my day!'

Behind me the bell went. It was time for lessons. I felt great. I turned to go. A little kid was standing in the doorway staring at me with an open mouth. What that kid must have thought he was looking at, I don't know.

He was seeing me being reborn.

'Thank you for hating me!' I yelled. I pushed him out of the way and I ran past him into the corridor. I felt like I'd just died and gone to heaven.

I was tested that day. I was tested hard. Word got about, see. Everyone knew what I had on underneath my school jumper. I got beat up again at break, but I didn't care. I just put my head down and hung on to the T-shirt and took it. It went on all day. I got pushed around in the corridor, people jeering, making threats. It didn't even bother me. There was nothing they could do to me that they hadn't already done. I knew something they would never know – that the very worst things in this world can turn into pure beauty, just by a single thought. It was a religious experience, a vision. Suddenly I understood what it was like to be a saint. Yes, I know the saints see God and all I'd seen was a

Metallica T-shirt, but so what? This was Me. This was who I was.

I tried to find Billie to tell her what was going on. I didn't know if she'd understand, but if anyone would it'd be her. She wasn't in that morning, though, so I just had to hug it to myself.

Davey came and found me at lunchtime. I was in a right state by then – covered in muck, tears in my eyes, my face all red from where I'd been slapped around.

First thing was – he'd found out who spat blackcurrant over me at the bus stop that morning.

'It was that kid, the one who was on at me about the snails yesterday. Him.'

Snailboy! That nosy little bog-wiping, smart-arsed snail-loving creep.

He was dead. It wouldn't be bullying, now – it'd be justice. Even a pacifist can only take so much.

Davey was staring at my face. 'You've still got it on under your jumper, haven't you? Take it off, Rob, take it off, won't you? You're going to get killed.'

'This is what I am, Davey,' I told him. Then I remembered. I had something to tell him. I'd decided – I was never going to let my brother down again. Now was as good a time as any.

'Mum gave it to me,' I said. He looked at me, like, he must have known. But I said it anyhow. 'She's gone, Davey, she's left him.'

Davey's little face just crumpled up. 'She can't have gone,' he said.

'We should be glad for her,' I told him. 'She's safe now. Remember, Davey – it's not us she's left. It's him. Always remember that.'

'You should have stopped her. You should have told her not to go!' he yelled suddenly, and before I could say any more he rushed off. I took a couple of steps after him, but he was too fast.

There was nothing I could have done. We both had to live with it from now on. I went off into the dining hall. Not much gets in the way of me and my dinner.

That's where it all came to a head.

I was standing by the sandwich stand when someone gave me a shove that sent me staggering into it – I almost knocked it down.

'I'm gonna have you, you pervert,' he sneered.

I just cracked. I'd had enough. You can't blame me. I mean, what was the point in hiding any longer? It was out – who I was, what I was and what I thought of all the idiots there with me. I was through with hiding. Hiding hadn't done me any good. People just see straight through it.

I ripped the jumper off over my head and stood there in all my Metallica motherfucking, fudge-packing, crack-smoking, Satan-worshipping glory. The T-shirt was ripped and filthy, I was covered in sweat and red-faced, tears in my eyes – I was crying like a little kid.

'Who wants a piece of me?' I bellowed. 'Come and get it, you bastards. Who wants it?'

And they did. They came at me in waves – kids and

staff all together. The first wave hit me. I lifted up my arm to fend them off.

'Thank you! Thank you . . .' I started to yell, but someone's elbow got my mouth and I went down in a blaze of glory.

Billie

The respite was OK. Mrs Grear. I've never been with her before. It was late by the time I got there. She just fed me and then I went to bed. The food was good – there was loads of it. Some of those places, they give you nothing, but this one was all right. She did me a big plate of beans and sausages, even though it was late.

'Keep you fed, anyhow,' she said.

I asked her if I was to come back to her the next night.

'As far as I know, love,' she said.

So it was all up in the air.

I had a long row of messages from Hannah when I turned my phone back on, asking me to call her, but I didn't answer. I wasn't in the mood for her. All I wanted to do was close my eyes and go to sleep, and send the world out of my mind.

I was hoping for a bit of a lie-in the next day, but it didn't happen. Mrs Grear woke me up at half seven. For some reason I was expecting to be out of school, but I wasn't. They can't have found out about the fight.

'Do you know the way from here?' she asked. I had no idea where I was, but it turned out I wasn't all that far from home. Shortcut through the park and I'd be on the main road.

It was good walking through the park that morning. Nice day, bit of sunshine. I was thinking it was a good thing I was out of Barbara and Dan's. It was always going to happen. And the school hadn't found out so far. You never know. Maybe I'd get to stay there.

I was just thinking maybe it was all going to be OK when I got jumped.

They knew what they were doing. There were four of them. The big one got me in a head lock and the others grabbed my arms and legs. They hauled me off into the bushes by the wall. The big one let go and pulled my head up by the hair to look in my face. I say big, I mean it. She was built like a sawn-off tree stump. She had a horrible snotty green cold, the skin all red around her squashed pig's nose, and her hair pulled back tight off her fat pig's face.

'I'm the queen now,' she said.

'What do you mean? There's no queen – it's just me, fatso,' I said, struggling. But they held me fast. Four of them. What can you do?

The big girl frowned. Perhaps I'd made it too complicated. Then she started to walk up and down, hawking. Did I mention she had a cold? She took her time at it, hawking and grieking, making sure she got a good load. Then she bent down, opened her mouth and coughed it at me.

Right in my face.

The next thing I know, I'm still in the grip of the sidekicks, but I must have nearly got out because some of them were the worst for wear. One had a bloody nose where I'd got her with my elbow or something.

'Get her, Betty, sort her out, quick, she's gonna get away!' someone was screaming.

Betty was standing there watching with her mouth open as if she couldn't believe it. Finally she closed her mouth into this hard little line, walked up, swung back her fist, which was about as big as a small dog, and hit me in the stomach.

I doubled up. All the air went out of me. They pulled me back upright and she did it again. Then they let go of me. There was that grim old bit when you're on the floor trying to catch your breath and twisting this way and that and the feet are going *bang bang bang*. Then they ran off.

They really did me. I thought I was going to suffocate. I must have looked as if I was having a fit, thrashing about on the grass trying to find some air. It felt like about half an hour before I got my breath back. It could have been worse. Sore ribs. Big red mark down one side of my face where someone had got me. My ear was bleeding where one of the bitches had stamped on my head, and I had one really sore tit. Like I say, it could have been worse. But not much. A little bit of my brain told me to get in touch with Hannah, but I was well past all that. She'd only talk me out of it and I wasn't having anyone talk me out of this.

No one jumps me like that.

*

I picked myself up and went back to Mrs Grear to get cleaned up. She was great – gave me a bath, rang the school telling them I was going to be late, and didn't mention that I'd been in a fight. I had the morning off in the end. I could have had the whole day, but I had business now, hadn't I?

I don't know what was going on at school that day – it was crazy. They'd already had one huge bundle in the hall, something to do with Rob. I told you, a kid like that, he just attracts trouble. Apparently he was wearing some kind of T-shirt he wasn't supposed to. They'd excluded him for bullying. Rob, bullying? They got that one wrong there.

I had a go at my form teacher, Mr Miles, about it.

'Rob doesn't bully – he gets bullied. What's going on?'

'He was wearing a T-shirt with some . . . inappropriate writing on it,' he said. 'The head asked him to take it off and he refused.' He shrugged, like that was an end to it.

'Oh, right, I get it,' I said. 'So what really happened is he gets beaten up for wearing the wrong clothes and then he gets excluded by you lot for wearing the wrong clothes. D'ya know what? You're no better than the kids.'

'Billie, I don't make the rules. It was really inappropriate.'

'Yeah, but you don't exclude someone for . . . oh, I can't be arsed with it.'

He yelled at me, but he was yelling at my back by

then. He knew better than to try and take it any further. The fact was I wasn't going to be there long, either. I was thinking, *See you at the Brant, Rob – if they let me back in, that is*. One thing for sure – they weren't going to have me back at Statside by the time this week was over.

Chris

It was Thursday. We were doing chairs. Wikes was drawing on the whiteboard again, a frog's kidney this time. I was planning on sneaking back in at break and writing 'Self Portrait' underneath it. I was looking forward to that. Pathetically, it was going to be the high point of my day.

I'd been in the tent for two nights so far. I had fish and chips the first night – that was OK. The night after, I went home with this kid Terry. He's a bit of a geek. I offered to let him show me his Wargames stuff. I was only going in for after-school snacks, but his mum asked me to dinner. It was weird, but it got me fed.

I was feeling good. I was on top of my game. I was sticking to the rules – my rules. I was going to school. I might have been prepared to bend that one if there was anywhere else to go to, but there never is, because everyone else is, well, at school. I was sitting tight, doing my work in class, not doing my homework at home. Perfectly reasonable.

It's just a pity they can't be reasonable as well.

Chairs is fun, though.

What you do is, while Wikes draws on the board, you and your mates stand up, grip the table in your hands and tiptoe off with it. You don't need to go far, just a metre or so to start with. The point is, when he looks round, the room has been rearranged. All done in total silence.

It's really funny.

The first time he didn't react at all. We'd all just tiptoed backwards with our tables a couple of metres, so we were all jammed up against the back wall. He might not have even noticed consciously. He just looked mildly surprised and got back to picking which colour pen to use next.

The second time we'd moved all the tables forward so we were all right up close to him. He spotted that all right. You could see him twitch.

The third time we were really subtle. We just turned our tables round so that we were all sitting there with our backs to him, staring at the wall opposite.

Wikes let out a terrible cry and flung his pen at us – it got Alex on the shoulder.

'Do you think I'm stupid? Do you think I don't know what's going on? You're going to stop this right now. Now! Now! I said NOW!' he screamed, and he banged his hand so hard on his desk it hurt him.

It was hilarious. Wikes was dancing around shaking his hurt hand. People were almost literally falling off their stools laughing. Even the good kids, the ones who like to pretend they're learning something from all his board dribble, even they were laughing. Wikes stopped dancing and just stood there looking at us falling about. Then he must have decided it just wasn't worth it and turned away and got back to doing his drawing on the board.

'This group . . .' he muttered, quietly. I was quite close to him. I think that's what he was saying. 'This group . . .' He had the pen up to the board, but he wasn't doing anything. Then, just for a moment, he rested his forehead against the board and it suddenly occurred to me he was hiding his face. Poor old Wikes, he was crying.

And then it wasn't funny any more.

It's one thing getting revenge for him being such a lazy arse, but I didn't want to make him cry. I hate bullies. It was the first time I thought to myself – maybe I was being one. Just because he was a teacher didn't mean he couldn't be bullied.

No one else had noticed. They were all hooting away like monkeys.

'Leave it out,' I hissed. 'He's upset – leave it.'

Alex and Jamie on my table went quiet and flapped their hands at the others so the noise died down. But Wikes must have heard me too, because he turned round, cool as anything. His eyes were red, so I knew I was right.

'Chris Trent,' he said to me in a quiet voice. 'I'll see you outside. Now. Go on.'

I got up and went out, with him right behind me. He was so quiet he scared me. I thought, *What now?*

Outside in the corridor, he came right up to me, so I

had to step back to keep my distance. He stepped further forward and put his hand on the wall so his arm was over my shoulder and leaned in close.

'You're the ringleader, Trent,' he said. 'Don't think I don't know.' He gulped a couple of times, trying to catch his words; he was still upset. 'School's wasted on the likes of you,' he said.

He was so close I could feel his breath on my face. I tried to move sideways, but he stepped round so he blocked my way. It was really uncomfortable.

'I was trying to stop it,' I pointed out, but he wasn't listening.

'Proud of yourself, I expect,' he said. 'Nothing better to do than make a mess for other people to clean up.'

'Sir . . .'

'Spoiling it for everyone else. You're just a little shit, Trent, aren't you?' he said.

I couldn't believe my ears at first. He said it so clearly there was no doubt, but I still couldn't believe it.

'What, sir?' I said.

'What, sir?' he mimicked. He pulled a face and shook his head. 'Your sort make me sick. A selfish little bastard, that's what you are. Your mother must be a right bitch to bring up something like you.'

'What?'

'You can stay there. I'll report this to the head.'

He turned to go. But – he can't say that! He can't get away with that!

I grabbed his shoulder. 'What did you say? What did you call my mother?' I hissed.

Wikes looked down at his shoulder and smirked. 'Assault is it now? I'll tell you what I said, Trent. Nothing. It's my word against yours. And we both know who'll be believed, don't we?'

I was so shocked. I just stood there staring at him. Where were the rules? Why was he doing this?

'If you don't get your grubby little hand off me right now, I'll get you done for assault. Because do you know what, Trent? There are plenty of other people in this school who'd like to see the back of you. Aren't there? Aren't there, Trent?'

'Yes, sir,' I said automatically, and I dropped my hand and looked away – just because I was ashamed at him speaking like that, I think.

Wikes nodded, and then he turned and walked back into the classroom. I stood and watched him like an idiot, because he'd treated me like scum and I'd still said yes sir no sir three bags full sir, like a good little boy. He closed the door quietly. Then I turned and went.

I was trying to stop it! All right, I do start it sometimes. If he wants to call me names, that's up to him – but he can't call my mother a bitch and get away with it, no way!

I was so angry. I stormed off down the corridor. I thought, *That's it. I've had enough of this crap now.*

I was going to go straight back to my tent, but I was taking a shortcut across the hall in front of the stage, and a teacher was coming in at the back and, you know what, I didn't want to explain myself, so I ducked up the stairs and behind the curtain and went to hide backstage.

It was Mrs Connelly. I heard her pause – she'd seen me go in – but she went on her way. Thought I was running an errand for someone, I expect.

I went to the little room backstage and sat down on the wicker costume basket. I had tears running down my face. It's funny, with me and school. It just goes on day after day. I get bored and I skive and I do what I can to avoid the work and punishments and things, and I get on with my life as much as I can. But really, it does my head in. I don't realize until something like this happens and suddenly there it is, right in my face.

I wanted to go home. I wanted just to forget about it. But what I wanted, more than anything, was to just tell someone how unfair it was that my crimes get pinned against me all the time while an idiot like Wikes, who makes so many people suffer every single day of his life, can call my mother a bitch and get clean away with it.

I started to have a look through the hamper of costumes. It was mainly panto stuff. The tutus were tiny – they must have been for Year 7s, I reckon. I had to split one up the sides to get it on and it only came down to just below my ribs. I have a hairy stomach. It looked ludicrous. I was starting to feel better.

Long stripy socks. Good. There was this pair of sequined pants, they were a bit small too, so I left my boxers on underneath. They left little to the imagination as it was. A tiara. A Superman cape. Then I raided the make-up table, spiked up my hair with gel, whitened out my face, did big blue eyes and a fat, smeary, ugly red trannie mouth.

Perfect.

I had to cover myself up with a coat on the way back to class – the last thing I wanted was to be hoiked off before I made my point.

I knocked on the door . . .

'Come in,' called Wikes.

I banged the door open and stood there in what I think is called a plié. Then I minced across the room, doing two or three turns as I did, and dived under Wikes's table.

The place exploded. Everyone was hooting and yelling. Wikes went mad. He tried to drag me out, but I'd got hold of the table legs.

'Get out! Get out! What do you think you're doing, boy? Get out!'

'I'm protesting,' I yelled back. 'I'm protesting against you calling my MOTHER A BITCH!'

The whole room went quiet when I said that. Wikes stood there, licking his lips for a moment. Then he nodded.

'Lying won't help you, Chris,' he said quietly. 'We'll see what the head has to say about it, shall we? Marion,' he told one of the girls. 'Go to fetch the headmaster, will you, please?'

He sat down on his chair and looked out of the window. The girl ran off out of the class. A minute or so passed, then I got out and went to sit on one of the desks while we waited for the head to show up.

Billie

I found out who the big girl was soon enough. Betty Milgram. She and her mates go to Langram High School, up the road from us. I knew what I was going to do before I'd finished wiping the snot off my face. She wants to play Queens. What does a queen do? She has an army, right?

This was war.

They get out at three at Langram's, earlier than us. So at half past two I got up and walked out the class. Mr Carradine can't do much.

'Where are you off to?' he said.

'It's time,' I called over my shoulder, not to him, to my mates. A bunch of them got up and walked out after me.

Carradine was standing there bleating, 'But it's not going-home time – the bell hasn't gone yet.'

'Just let them go, sir,' said one of the other kids. No one came after us. Glad to see the back of us, I expect.

I went down the corridor yelling, 'It's time!' I was

only after a handful of kids from my year, but other kids were leaving too. Word had got about. It was great, better than I ever expected. People started diving into other classes shouting, 'Fight! Fight at Langram's. Billie's having a fight.' Even classes that weren't anything to do with it came out. By the time we got out into the road we must have had at least fifty and there were more behind us running out of the gates. There were teachers trying to head them off, but by then it was a stampede.

We were going to war. I was expecting the police to turn up at any time – I thought someone'd ring them – but they never showed till later. We lost a few on the way, but there were still twenty or thirty of us by the time we arrived. I was out in front. It was my fight. I took off my school tie and wrapped it round my head. I didn't plan it. It was only later I thought – *Rambo*. You know, the bandanna round his head? I used to watch those films with Mum on the TV when I was little.

As we got close to the gates and spotted the Langram uniforms we broke into a run. My lot – my army – they were right behind me. I turned and waved my hand. We charged. Yea! The Langrams turned and ran for it. We let out another yell and speeded up – yeeee-hay! Oh, man! I was so full of it. All that crap, school, home, sod that. This is what it's all about.

We closed in, howling and yelling. The Langram kids were getting jammed in the gate where they'd all tried to run back in at the same time. Trapped like rats, nowhere to run. We ran right up into the wedge in the gate and started on 'em straight off. We were shoving and kicking at them for a few minutes before some of the bigger ones, my age, came round the back and then the battle started proper. I remember someone coming behind me and pulling my hair. I spun round and smacked her hard round the earhole. Down she went, yelling and clutching her ear, silly cow. I could have had her nose all over her face if I wanted.

You should have seen it! It was fantastic. Everyone jumping on everyone else. And it was all mine. My own private war. I had a group around me, the hard ones, Jane O'Leary and Sue Simpson, my deputies. There were fights everywhere, little groups of kids all over the playground and spilling out the gates. Then I saw her – Betty, with her little group of thugs. They'd just turned the corner by the front entrance. I let out a whoop and went running with Sue and Jane after me. Three against four – good odds.

Betty screwed up her big ugly face when she saw me coming. She clenched her fists and her little piggy eyes swivelled from side to side. Nowhere to run, fat girl, trapped by your own friends clustered up behind you. She was going to get spanked and she knew it. I was going to teach all four of them a lesson.

'Kill the bitches!' I screamed, and Jane and Sue let out a yelp by my side. We went in, I had to jump up at Betty to get my head anywhere near her fat snotty nose, but I felt it crunch lightly, that soft crunch you get, when you know you've broken something inside.

PART 2

The Brant

Chris

I was held in custody by the head until my parents arrived, so they could all 'discuss' my future. Not one of them believed a word I said. They swallowed the Wikes version hook, line, sinker, rod, fisherman, the lot.

He lied. He stood there and lied and lied and lied. He avoided looking at me the whole time, but I finally caught his eye at the end of it, and the two-faced old toad gazed straight back at me. Not a flicker. As if it was me who was full of poisonous bullshit – as if it was me who'd insulted his mother and got away with it.

'And even if we did believe you,' said my dad after, 'my sympathies are still with Mr Wikes.'

I was excluded for two weeks and sent to the PRU – the Pupil Referral Unit. If it happened again, the head said, I'd be out permanently.

'See where he's headed?' said my father to my mother on the drive home. 'It starts off with refusing to work; it ends with him shoving teachers around in the corridor.'

'I'm amazed at you, Chris,' said Mum. 'It's not like you at all. What's got into you?'

'I told you – he was lying. He called you a bitch,' I said. 'I stood up for you. Don't you even care?'

'Just – stop it, Chris. I can't bear this deceit.' She shook her head and scowled in the mirror.

'They won't stand for any of your games at Brant PRU, I can tell you that now,' declared my dad triumphantly.

See what you're up against? It's like a police state. If you think for yourself, every man's hand is against you. I told them exactly what was going on, clear as a bell, but I might as well have been blowing bubbles for all the attention they were paying me.

You can trust no one. Your teachers, your parents – they're all just gagging to turn you in just for the hell of it.

Even your best friend.

This is going to be a nasty shock to anyone who believes in such concepts as 'friendship', and 'loyalty', and so on. I was planning to hang around for a few hours, then slip out back down to my camp site. But my supposed best friend, Alex Higgs, revealed the whereabouts of my tent to his mother that evening. Apparently she convinced him it was for my own good. That was a bitter moment, when they told me that.

Result? I was trapped at home over the entire weekend where my parents could do exactly as they liked. It was a relief, to be honest, when Monday morning came and I had to go to Brant PRU. Or, as my dad put it, 'the educational rubbish tip'.

I had both of them drop me off in the car. Double supervision. I think it was finally dawning on Mum that I wasn't ever shifting on the homework front, whereas Dad was still going mad with rage at the thought of having an academic under-achiever in the family.

'What is it with you about doing well at school?' I asked him. 'You did well at school and where did it get you?'

'What about me? I've got a good job, haven't I?' he said.

'Yes, but you hate it,' I pointed out.

'That's not the point,' he spluttered. 'I had the option.'

'The option to be miserable? No thanks.'

He's so convinced he's right that he is honestly unable to imagine that I might actually believe what I say. I. Don't. Want. To do well. At school. What part of that is hard to understand? Is that what education does to you? Makes you stupid? Thanks, I'd rather hang on to my native gifts, if it's all the same to you.

He was that angry with me. I wish I had a camera – it would have made a great reality TV show, except no one would believe it. As they dropped me off at the Brant, he started banging his head histrionically, but lightly, against the steering wheel.

'My son. In with the losers,' he groaned hollowly.

'The kids here aren't losers,' my mum snapped at him. 'They just have problems, the same as other people.'

'Problems?' Dad glared at her. 'What problems does he have?' he said, jerking his head to the loser in the back of the car. 'Broken marriage? Poverty? He's not disadvantaged – he's just lazy.'

'That doesn't make him a loser,' said Mum tensely.

I could only see the back of her head so I never saw the danger signals, but I sensed them anyway. I reached gently over to open the door. 'I'd better –' I began, but she began lift-off before I finished.

'How dare you speak like that in front of your own son?' she yelled suddenly at Dad. 'A loser . . . I can't believe I'm hearing this.'

'I don't see why not,' snarled Dad. 'It's been staring you in the face for long enough. And now look at us. You're letting him undermine our whole marriage.' He laughed bitterly. 'Let's get some perspective on this. Am I the one who's failed my education?'

'Don't call him failed!'

'What else do you want me to call him? Succeeded?'

'He's fifteen years old! How can he be failed, you idiot?' roared Mum back at him. But I'd heard enough. I opened the door.

'Bye,' I called softly.

'Wait there,' snapped Mum, but they were both at it so hard they hardly noticed me stepping out. I closed the door quietly – best not to attract attention from the ravening beast when it's in the middle of its, its what, its anti-mating display. There were a group of rough-looking kids smoking just a few metres away, looking at me as if I was made out of pure, undiluted, grammar-school nerd. I was. To make matters worse, they had their ordinary clothes on and I was in uniform. Did that mean . . . no! It was your own clothes here . . . ?

I was going to be the only one in school uniform. It wasn't going to be nice.

Well, I thought, *if they want a punch-up, they can have one*. I'd give them some fat grammar-school fist to taste if they liked.

I walked smartly up to the door, and I was just reaching out to press the button to get attention when Mum noticed I was gone. I heard the car door go behind me and her feet on the pavement. I tried to dodge out of the way, but she seemed to teleport or something. She had hold of me in a bosomy embrace before I could even turn round. Out of the corner of my eye I could see the crowd of smoking kids watching with interest.

'Darling!' she bellowed.

NO, I silently begged . . . *please not 'darling'!* She squidged me into her heaving bosom and gave me a huge hug. Right there. On the pavement. In front of Brant PRU.

'I don't care what your father says. You're a star. You'll always be a star to me,' she said breathlessly. 'This is just a temporary setback, that's all. Fifteen years old and a loser. As if!' she said, giving me a brave smile.

I glanced over at the kids who had started smirking as well as smoking. Mum kissed me once more for luck, then hurried back. I stood and watched as the car began shaking as she climbed in. I could hear them shouting at each other before he got the engine going again, and proceeded to jerk, stall and grind the gears all the way up the road and out of sight.

And there he was, not five minutes before, telling me I didn't come from a disadvantaged background.

I pressed the intercom and while I was waiting for an answer, a girl turned up. She was a little shorter than me, in jeans and a leather jacket, short black hair, quite pretty, nice figure, but she looked as if she'd been in a small war – her face was bruised, her lips were puffed up and she had an eye as black as a rotten plum. I thought, *Oh my God. And this is what they do to girls here*.

'Sorry,' muttered the girl. She leaned on the bell again, and looked me up and down.

I smiled. She didn't smile back. She scowled. It was the biggest scowl I'd ever seen.

The door buzzed. The girl pushed it open and I followed her up the stairs to the reception. As soon as she saw the girl in the leather jacket, the receptionist came running out and put her arms round her.

'There, love,' said the woman. 'At least we'll be seeing more of you. Now,' she went on, getting her eye on me. 'I know Hannah wants to see you upstairs. You go up while I deal with this young man here.'

The girl left, and the woman turned to me. 'Welcome to the Brant,' she said. 'I'm Melanie,' and she held out her hand for me to shake.

It wasn't very receptionist-type behaviour. She got

me to sign their agreement about how to behave and then she called the head, who turned out to be a bloke called Jim. I thought, *Jim? Jim the bloke? Jim the headmaster bloke? What's this about, then?*

'I'll give you the lowdown later, have a proper chat,' Jim told me. 'All you need to know now is – this is a safe place. People come here for all sorts of reasons; they're in all sorts of trouble. But trouble is left out there.' He jerked his thumb over his shoulder. 'In here, we all respect one another. If you have any problems, come to me. And above all – no fights. Safe place. OK?'

'Suits me,' I said.

'Good. Now – let's go and meet the others.'

Jim bloked his way down the corridor and I followed after him. He had the old blokiness thing off to a T, Jim had. I wasn't in the same blokey league.

'Had some breakfast, Chris?' he said, leading the way down the corridor. 'We do toast, we do cereal, usually, unless it's all been troughed. We can only afford so much each week.'

'Yeah, I had some, but, I mean, I could eat some more,' I muttered.

We came out at a breakfast bar . . . the assembly area he called it. A few kids were sitting around – all dressed in their own clothes. As I thought. Only me in uniform. I was a geek, right from the start.

Jim poured me a glass of apple juice.

'Welcome to Brant PRU,' he said. He got another one for himself and toasted me – cheers. 'This is Chris, our new intake. Make him welcome, will you.'

One of the girls scowled at him. 'Why don't you get me a glass of juice?' she asked.

'I was being nice to him,' said Jim. 'Remember that, Ruth – being nice to people?' Ruth didn't look impressed.

'Why can't you be nice to me?'

'I'm nice to you all the time. It's your turn to be nice to me now,' said Jim. He smiled, a big broad smile at Ruth, then he left us to it.

I sipped my juice and watched carefully.

'Why're you dressed like that?' asked one kid, an Asian lad.

'No one told me, did they? I must look a right freak,' I grumbled, trying to make light of it.

'We're all freaks here, pal,' said the girl called Ruth. 'Failures, geeks, the too tall, the too short, the too clever, the not clever enough. That's us.'

'Yeah?' I said. I was wondering how many of the other kids agreed with that.

'Welcome to the zoo,' she added. 'This is Jess,' she said, introducing a pale girl sitting next to her. 'She doesn't say much, but she's my mate, right, Jess? And this is Ed. He's the most irritating kid in the world, according to Jim, and he may even be right.'

The kid called Ed smiled proudly at me.

'This is Maheed. He's a terrorist,' she said.

The Asian kid laughed. 'Knock it off, Ruth,' he said.

I raised my cup to take another sip of juice and Ed – the most irritating kid in the world, Ed – nudged my elbow so the drink went down my front.

'Hey, what did you do that for?'

'He was being irritating,' said Maheed. 'He does it all the time.'

Ed nudged my arm again. The juice slopped over the edge of the cup.

'I'm going to have to smack him,' I pointed out.

'You can't hit him. It's a safe place in here,' said Ruth. 'That can get you chucked out, and if you get chucked out of here it's the LOK.'

'What's the LOK?' I asked, but before anyone could reply Ed nudged my arm again and more juice slopped over the edge of the cup.

'Can I throw my drink at him instead?' I asked.

'Yeah,' said Ruth. So I did. Right in his smirky little face.

'Sir, sir, look what the new boy's done! Sir . . .' wailed Ed, and he ran out towards Jim's office.

'Sorry,' said Ruth. 'I should have said no.' And they all bent over and started killing themselves laughing.

Hannah

Billie Trevors. First thing on a Monday morning. Trouble.

Billie's not trouble to me because she's so bad. She's not even trouble because she's one of those kids I can't relate to. She's trouble because she's one of those kids I can't stop relating to.

The first time I saw her, I thought, *That can't be her*. They'd all been going on about what a monster she was, the fights, the beatings she'd given. And then in comes this girl, scowling away like Dennis the Menace, this black cloud hanging over her. Well, I'd seen that scowl before. That wasn't anger. That was her way of trying not to cry. So, you see, Billie broke my heart the first time I saw her. Then I read her history and she broke my heart all over again, and she's been breaking it ever since.

You can't let that happen in this line of work. You can love 'em in the office but not at home, my old supervisor told me. But there's always a back door to your heart, isn't there? And Billie will find a way whether you want her there or not.

Billie has to be hard because she's so soft. It's the only way she can survive. That's why she breaks my heart. In that little girl beats the biggest heart you'll ever find. If only people knew. If only *she* knew.

That's what I'm for. To try and show her that inside she's brimming over with love.

She came in, white as a sheet. Scowling away like the devil. Trying not to cry.

'Welcome back, Billie,' I said. I didn't go and hug her – not yet. I can imagine how she felt – she'd just blown everything we'd been working towards in the space of twenty-four hours. But I wouldn't be doing my job if I ran round the table to hug her straight off, would I?

'So.' I ruffled up her notes. 'You really hit the jack-pot this time,' I said. 'Lost your foster home and excluded from school in just one day. It's got to be a record.'

She gave me a half smile. 'You told me if I had to fight, keep it out of school. So I did . . . out of my school anyway,' she said.

'Don't be clever, Billie. I didn't tell you to start the Third World War, did I? According to this there were over fifty kids involved.'

'That many?' She laughed.

'Well, Billie, I don't find it funny. Three people were hospitalized during your little bit of fun, one of them quite seriously. How do you feel about that?'

She pulled a face. I was genuinely annoyed. It's one

thing to get carried away, to lose it. But she'd been planning this all that day.

'Sorry,' she said. I waited. That wasn't what I asked her. 'Not good,' she said at last. She tried to meet my eye, but couldn't.

I hadn't finished yet. 'It's what you wanted, to come back here, isn't it? Is that what this was about? Are you taking a chance on Jim letting you in?'

'No! I was trying. I was cutting down on the fights. I was on a diet.'

'Billie, a fight diet is still fighting.'

'It's not easy. They all want a pop because I have a reputation.'

I relented a little. Gave her a sympathetic smile. 'Yeah, Billie the Kid, that's you.'

'Billie the bloody Kid,' she said, and she pulled the most terrible scowl you ever saw. It almost bent her face in half. It was that hard for her not to cry.

I expect you thought I was being nice to her when I made that little Billie the Kid joke. Well, I wasn't. If there's one sure-fire way to get to Billie, be nice to her when she's in trouble. She can't bear it.

'So what happened at home?' I asked, when she looked as if she could speak again.

She was furious again at the mere thought. 'The stupid cow only got an armed-response unit round! Can you believe that? An armed-response unit! For God's sake!'

'Billie, she must have been really scared to do that.'

'She had no business. I did what you said. When I felt myself losing it I went upstairs.'

'So what went wrong?'

'She said . . . she said about my mum . . .' said Billie, and her little face bent in half again.

A thought. Where are we – end of April?

'It's her birthday about now, isn't it?'

Billie stared at me, eyes brimming over, utterly unable to speak. I checked my notes. Mum's birthday the week before.

Oh, Billie.

'Did you see her, love?'

Billie shook her head and glared.

'Ah, love.' She can cope with a lot, but say anything against her mum and she's gone. It was her mum's birthday and she never even saw her.

No kid should have to put up with hearing their mum being slagged off, especially by their carer, but you just can't blow up like that because someone says things, no matter what they say. 'Mrs Barking shouldn't have said things about your mum, Billie, but it's still no excuse for going off like that,' I told her. 'You scare people, Billie, and scared people go for right for where it hurts. You have to learn to walk away from it.'

Billie scowled. 'Yeah, it's always me that has to walk away, isn't it? Anyhow, there's nothing to walk away from now. She chucked me out, didn't she?'

'Barbara hasn't said she won't have you back.'

Billie's eyes bulged. 'After what she did to me? Put me in the nick? Had the armed police out after me? I wouldn't stay with her again if it was the last place on earth.'

'Billie . . .'

'Forget it! She's a lying bitch!'

'No.'

'She tells lies!'

'No . . .'

'She does!'

'What happened last time, when you smashed that window in and punched him, what's his name . . .'

'Dan.'

'Dan. You punched him in the nose.'

'I broke it 'n'all.'

'. . . because she . . .'

'Because she lashed out at me, the cow. She had a go first – don't forget that!'

'So you broke Dan's nose . . .'

'I should have done hers. It was her asking for it, not him.'

'And what happened?'

'No . . .'

'What happened? What did she say after? Well?'

Billie started writhing around in her seat. She knew where this was going. 'She said sorry,' she growled eventually.

'She said sorry. OK, listen. You promised not to have any more fights . . .'

'People keep having a go! At least two of those fights I was stopping other kids from having a go at this new kid.'

'No difference. Mrs Barking is at the end of her tether, Billie. You've smashed your room, how many times? Four, five in the last year? You swore on everything that's holy, no more fights, and you're still having loads. So, yes, she loses it every now and then and goes a bit over the top . . .'

'Over the top? Goes hysterical!'

'Yeah, all right, hysterical. And do we know anyone else like that? Someone sitting right here in this room, for instance, who has a tendency to overreact? And beat people up and smash things to pieces. Fair bit worse than her, I'd say.'

Billie stared at me with her face as white as chalk, at the sheer effrontery of being put in the same class as Barbara Barking.

'And despite all this,' I went on, 'she still hasn't chucked you out. What does that show? Come on, Billie, tell me – what does that show?'

Billie, who had been writhing about, slapping the table and kicking her feet, slumped down in her chair. Her eyes were like pools of tar.

'What does it show, Billie?'

'Commitment,' she whispered.

'Commitment. Right.'

I waited a bit while she got herself together.

'You're a hard person to live with, Billie – you know that. She overreacts – you know that. But she wants you back. She must love you to do that. So cut her some slack, will you?'

'I'm not going back there!'

'You don't want to go back because it's easier to run away. But this is what it's about – going forward with what you've got. So. You'll go, right.'

Another long wait. At last, though, she nodded. 'But I don't want to, right?'

'Good girl, Billie. You are getting there.'

'How can you say that? I screwed everything up,' she moaned, and then the tears began.

'She wants you back. You're trouble, but she knows you're worth it. That's because you *are* worth it, Billie.'

Billie pulled one of her ugliest faces – and she has some beauties. But she didn't deny it.

'So,' I went on. 'That's one good thing that's come out of all this, Billie. And another one is – have you seen Jim?' I asked her.

'No, I came straight up.'

'You better go and have a word as soon as we're done here. You're not supposed to be back in here after what happened last time – you know that.'

She stared at me, scared out of her life. 'Am I down the LOK?' she begged.

She'd had enough. I shook my head. 'No. No, you're not. You will be if anything happens again, Billie. There's only so much he can do.'

'Oh, top! He's letting me back in?'

'He's putting his neck out for you, Billie.'

'Oh, that's great – I thought I was down the LOK. He won't regret it and you won't neither. Honest, I'll be so good, I really will.'

'Billie – the fights have to stop. I mean, really. No diets. A total, complete stop. All you have to do is lift one finger to anyone in this building and you're out so fast you'll get skid marks on your underpants. Right?'

She nodded. 'I know you've all put your necks out for me, letting me back in. I'm really grateful.'

Time for a little encouragement. 'You *are* doing well, Billie. But you have to go just that little bit further.'

'I like it here. You know that.'

'Right, then. No fights. Do we have a deal?'

She nodded. But . . . I don't know. It was like she was losing interest. She started twisting in her chair and biting her nails and looking around.

'What?' I asked her. She shook her head. 'No, tell me. What's the problem?'

Billie looked at me and pulled a face. 'Time for a little encouragement, wasn't it?' She watched me dither – she's so sharp, that girl! 'Yeah, I know,' she went on. 'I've done all those personal-development sessions – I know what you're doing. And you know what, Hannah? You're good at it. You get me on track and make me feel more in charge of myself. But – you do it for me, and then you do it for the next kid who comes through the door as well. And the next kid, and the next and the next. And if a better job offer comes, you'll move. You'll go. They all go in the end and you're no different, are you? I don't blame you,' she added when I tried to speak. 'Why should I blame you for taking the trouble? It's good of you. It's just that – that's as good as it's going to get for me, isn't it? A good professional. That's what you are. A good professional. Aren't you?'

Oh, Billie.

I nodded. 'I hear what you're saying,' I said. 'I know I'm not your mum and I'm not your family and I never will be. I'll tell you what, though, Billie. No, Billie, no, look at me . . .'

She was turning her head and getting up to leave. And suddenly, suddenly, I was furious. Furious for her – I'm used to that. Furious with her – I was used to that too. But this time I was furious with myself for some reason. Don't ask – I don't understand it myself. I didn't even know what I was doing or what I was going to say. I ran round the table and grabbed hold of her and spun her round to face me.

'Don't touch me!' she yelled. She flushed red and I knew I was in trouble, but I wasn't going to stop, not now.

'You listen . . . you listen . . . Billie! Billie!' She was doing her best to get away and I had to grab her in both hands. I'm no fighter. She could have floored me, but she didn't. That's all the encouragement I had, but I went on.

'You will hear me. Because I AM going to be here for you. This is personal. I'm not going anywhere until you're back on your feet, not for money and not for love. Do you understand me, Billie?'

She was seething, crying, raging, I don't know. She shoved me away and turned to go again, but I dragged her back.

'Don't you dare turn your back on me! Don't you bloody dare! I do believe in you. Do you understand? I'm not. Letting. You. Go.'

There was a pause. Billie was panting. Her face had gone as white as a sheet. And you know what? I was the one who was crying.

I let go of her to wipe my eyes.

'There, look what you've done now,' I said. I dabbed at my eyes and wiped them on my sleeve, there were tears everywhere. Billie stood there glaring at me. Dennis the bloody Menace. I knew she was fighting as hard as she could not to cry, not to run and not to tear me to pieces all in one go. One of them was going to happen and at that moment, neither of us knew which it was going to be.

'I've never said that to anyone before, not to any man, not to anyone,' I told her. 'So don't you let me down. Don't you dare. Don't you bloody dare let me down!'

Billie stood there heaving a moment longer, then she turned and ran out of the room, slamming the door. The whole room shook. I stood there trying to catch my breath. I mean – unprofessional or what? Jim would kill me if he found out I'd said that to one of the kids.

I went back to my desk to try and clean myself up. I don't wear much make-up, so it wasn't such a disaster, but even so it was a few minutes before I felt fit to face the world. I was just getting better, when the door creaked open.

'Hello?' I called. No one appeared.

That door's never done that before.

'Hello?' I called again. 'Billie?'

There was no reply. Cautiously, I went over to have a look. The door opened a little more until I could see a hand just holding it open. I got close and then stopped.

And a voice – the tiniest, tiniest little voice you ever heard – whispered to me.

'I love you, Hannah.'

And then I took another step . . . and then there were feet running away up the corridor.

I ran to the door, just in time to see her running round the corner. 'Billie!' I shouted. 'I love you too!' But she wasn't there to hear it.

There was a kid in the corridor staring at me. I grinned like an idiot and stepped back into the office.

I was that close!

Yeah, well, maybe. But with Billie I've often felt that. She's right there, in the palm of my hand – and I close my hand and she's gone. She can love – she can't stop herself loving. But she can't ever believe that anyone can really love her back. That's her problem. Not loving – being loved. She has to let herself into someone's heart. Until she can do that, she's always going to be in danger. Prison. Suicide. Drugs. Prostitution. They're all there waiting for her. There are so many hands reaching out for her. So many people want a girl like Billie, and she just cannot work out which are the right ones.

Rob

Guess what? I've been up to my old tricks again. Bullying. Funny. I never realized that's what was happening when I was under a heap of twenty kids all kicking the shit out of me. It just goes to show how wrong you can be. But that's what the head says, so it must be true.

'We do not tolerate bullying in this school.'

I told him there'd been dozens of them and just one of me, so how's that bullying? Then he asked me to take the T-shirt off and I said no and he said yes and I said no . . .

And that was that. I was out. And then he rang home.

It was all right up to then. Being beat up by all those kids – fine. Having my T-shirt christened by the hordes of hell – fantastic! Getting sent out of school – no problem. Sitting there watching the head talking to Philip on the phone – miserable. The magician of shit strikes again.

You have to hand it to Philip. He is the best magician of shit who has possibly ever lived. I'd just been through a miracle. I'd been reborn. I'd discovered how to turn the worst things you can imagine into pure gold. But not Philip. He didn't have to be there. I didn't even have to hear his voice. Just watching someone talking to him on the phone was enough. When the head dialled, I was a hero; by the time he put the phone back down I had turned back into shit. From shit to gold and back to shit again in the space of one morning. Yep. Philip really knows his stuff.

He didn't come and pick me up from school, that was one thing, but I still had to go home to him and face the music. He was sitting in front of the telly when I got in. He called me in.

'I'm sorry,' I said.

'So am I,' he said. Then he waved me away upstairs, and just as I was going out, he said . . .

'Little drummer boy,' he said, and he shook his head. He calls me that sometimes, ever since he took away my drums. He says it like it means he's fond of me. Mum used to call it that – a term of endearment, she used to say. I never thought that, though.

'Oh, and, Robbie,' he said.

'Yeah.'

'Take that T-shirt off.'

And I said, 'No.'

He turned to look round at me. I stood and looked at him for a moment. Then I left him to it.

I was late to the Brant on my first day. I got there at break. Melanie on the desk went through the rules with me and asked me to sign an agreement – you know the sort of thing – treat one another with respect and so on yadi yada. Then out popped Jim Stanley, the head or dep or whatever he is.

'Welcome to the Brant, Robbie,' he said, and then he looked me up and down and he said, 'Did you read the rules? You didn't happen to notice the one about hoodies?'

Oh, man! No hoodies. I was hoping that was one of those rules that no one bothered with. It wasn't that I was hung up on the hoodie. The only trouble was . . .

'I have to ask you to take it off, Robbie,' he said.

'You don't really want me to take it off,' I said.

'Oh, I do.'

So I did.

I could hear Melanie gasp behind me at about the same time as Jim gasped. By this time the T-shirt was about as metal as a T-shirt can get. Blood, spit, mud – you name it. It was ripped. It was filthy in every way possible. That T-shirt had been through more than I had.

It was great.

Melanie leaned round behind my head. 'Turn round, Robbie,' she said. I turned round. I could feel the words burning into my back.

CRACK-SMOKING
FUDGE-PACKING
SATAN-WORSHIPPING
MOTHERFUCKER

'You better come into my office,' said Jim.

*

He was very calm about it, Jim, I'll give him that.

'You know we have rules, Robbie,' he said. Then he paused and had a closer look. 'What happened to it? It's horrible.'

'I got beat up in it,' I said proudly.

'The report said you'd been fighting.'

'I wasn't fighting. The T-shirt was,' I said, and I eyeballed him to see how he'd take it. The signs didn't look good. 'My mum gave it to me,' I added.

'Does your mum know the trouble you're in?' he asked.

'No.'

'How come?'

'She left.'

'Oh? And when was this, Robbie?'

I didn't reply to that. It wasn't actually any of his business.

Jim shook his head. 'OK,' he said. 'Let's get down to it. Whatever's going on at home, there are still rules. Everywhere has rules, that's life, and we're no exception. There's a rule about hoodies. Not everyone gets that one. Some of the staff have issues with it, to be honest. Maybe I have a bit of a thing about it. I expect I have. But, there it is, it's a rule and we have to stick to it.'

'I don't have any trouble not wearing a hoodie.'

'Good. Now. That thing.' He pointed at the T-shirt. 'That has to come off too.'

'Not going to happen,' I said.

'Rob.'

'No way.'

'Rob.'

'Sorry.' I stood up. 'Do I have to go now.'

'Where to? The LOK?'

'If I have to.'

Even Philip hadn't been able to make me take that T-shirt off. What was the LOK after Philip?

Jim shook his head. 'Robbie, I want you to stay here. Sit down. Let's see if we can work this out.'

'I don't have to take it off, then?'

'I said, sit down and let's see if we can work it out. I didn't say we *can* work it out, but we can try. Now, please . . . sit down.'

I paused, but . . . at least it was a conversation and not a bawling. That's a start. I sat down. Jim looked at me for a bit.

'Cup of tea?' he said.

'Can I have coffee?' I asked.

He stuck his head out of the office and bawled, 'Melanie! One tea, one coffee, please.'

'Coming!'

He sat back and looked at me.

'I suppose we could lend you a top. The trouble is if you get hot . . .'

'I can put up with being hot.'

'The real trouble is it's another rule, isn't it? You can't go around with that stuff written on you. What if someone lifts your top up? How did it kick off at school?'

'Someone lifted my top up,' I admitted.

He nodded. He had another think. 'OK. Tell you what. I have kids with stuff as bad – well, almost as bad – tattooed on their skin, and they don't get sent back. So there is a precedent. How about if you put it on inside out? We'll lend you another top. Then if it does ride up or something, no one will see.'

I had a think about it. It wasn't bad. It was quite clever, really. It was still hiding my true self, though.

'It's how I am,' I told him, holding the shirt out for him to see. 'It's *me*.'

'Rob. You have to work with me on this one.'

I thought a bit more, then I nodded. Give him credit, eh? He was trying, which was more than all the other bastards who'd tried to make me take it off.

'I can live with that,' I said.

'Great.' Jim got up and bawled out for Melanie to get me a top. 'Extra large, please,' he added, eyeing me up. 'One other thing,' he said. 'It needs a wash.'

'This is me,' I said.

'You need a wash too.'

'I'll have a think about it,' I said.

'Just don't think about it too long. OK?'

'OK.'

I had my coffee, turned the T-shirt inside out, put on the top they lent me and went through to the assembly area. It was a good idea, actually, wearing the T-shirt inside out. It felt safe, which was something I'd not felt for the last day or so. I was feeling a bit better. I got through to the assembly area – and guess what? Who do I find sitting there, sipping his morning cuppa like he owned the place? Only the revolting little mollusc who started the whole thing off. Snailboy himself.

I couldn't believe it. The guy was haunting me.

He looked up at me and trembled. 'Hi,' he squeaked.

'What are you doing here?' I demanded.

'Same as you, I expect,' he said. Smart arse.

'I doubt that.' I reached down, just to show him who was boss here, pinched his bit of toast and started munching it.

'Oi!' This was one of the girls. 'I made that for him,' she said.

'He just gave it to me,' I said.

I know – I know! But this was the kid who threw Ribena on the sacred T-shirt. Fair's fair. I owed him a big, fat bullying.

The girl was annoyed. 'Don't you go starting trouble round here,' she snapped.

'He's different,' I said.

'Doesn't matter,' she said. 'We don't have fights in here.'

I shrugged. 'You're still dead, mate,' I told Snailboy. 'I have to get him back for gobbing juice all over me from the bus,' I explained to the girl.

'Did you?' she asked him. He admitted it was true. 'Oh well,' she said. 'You deserve it, then.'

Result!

And then . . . I mean, I was winning. I was on top. I almost had permission to wipe the floor with his grinning snaily face when . . . guess who came in? Only

Billie. She hadn't been at school the morning of the miracle. It was the first time I'd seen her since she saved my bacon from Riley.

'Billie!' I called, and I ran over to her. She was only a few steps away. She half turned when she heard my voice, and I think she started to smile. And then I was falling. I don't know what happened – something hit my feet and I was going down fast. I grabbed out to save myself and I caught hold of Billie by the waist. No, worse. I grabbed her by the trousers.

Can you believe that? This is my life? How could it be that I grabbed hold of Billie Trevors's trousers? And how did it happen that they came down? Right down round her ankles. There was this gasp in the room and the next thing I remember I was on my back being hit from every direction at the same time. I was being beaten up by at least five people dancing round me putting the boot in.

'Don't . . . don't . . . don't . . .' she was going. And the foot, everywhere. Face, belly, nuts . . .

Then – don't ask why, I have no idea – Snailboy jumped in. 'Eh, go on, that's enough,' he yelled, like Batman or something, the idiot. Billie wasn't listening. Snailboy grabbed her from behind and pulled her off. I rolled into a corner and clambered to my feet, just in time to see the whole thing. It was beautiful, what she did to Snailboy. Like a dance. She banged his hands so he let go of her and chopped him on the neck, all in one smooth movement. She stepped back lightly to let him fall down to the ground. Then she lifted up her foot and stamped, once, very hard. Very very hard. Right on the nuts.

You could hear the thudding noise as her foot sank home. Snailboy didn't say a word, he just grunted, but you could see his face changing colour. Then Jim came running in, and Melanie and this woman from upstairs, to see what was going on.

'Billie! That's enough!' yelled the woman.

Billie looked up. You never saw anyone look so angry in all their life. It was the scowl of death. It was my death. I cringed into the corner. I was thinking, *Please, Billie, don't kill me, please! Please, Billie, not my balls, please.*

But it was over. Billie let out this weird yell and ran out of the door. Jim bent down over the remains of Snailboy.

'Chris! Are you all right?' Outside there was a tremendous banging – Billie, trying to kick her way out of the locked door.

'Let her out. She's done here,' said Jim.

The woman from upstairs ran after her. On the floor, Snailboy let out a long, slow moan of the most terrible agony. You knew – he just wanted to die.

'Call an ambulance,' called Jim to Melanie. 'Just in case.' He bent down to Snailboy. 'It's all right, son, it'll pass. Nothing to worry about,' he said.

Nothing to worry about except his balls. I wondered if he'd ever be able to have kids after that – I swear I heard something pop when her foot came down.

It should have been me.

'I can fight my own fights,' I heard some wanker shouting. I wasn't surprised to realize it was me. I thought, *I'm out of here. I've blown this just about as much as it's possible to blow anything and I don't seem to be able to stop myself.*

'I still owe you,' I snarled at the poor bastard writhing about on the floor. Then I legged it out of the door. They let me go. I didn't think anyone was going to want to see me back there in a hurry. I paused on the stairs to make sure Billie wasn't waiting for me, but it was all clear – she was halfway down the road by then. I legged it.

Everything was getting worse and worse and there was no way of stopping it.

Chris

Everything turned blinding white, then blinding red, then black, then blinding white again. The colours of pain. I couldn't believe anything could hurt so bad. And then, when Jim asked for an ambulance, I couldn't believe that either.

'I don't need an ambulance,' I groaned. But I did. It was just a wish. 'Am I going to be all right?' I asked. What I really wanted to say was, 'Will I ever be able to have sex?' But I didn't dare.

'It's all right – it's just in case,' someone kept saying. But I knew, I knew. They would say that, wouldn't they? I was going to wake up tomorrow with no balls. And I hadn't even got to use them properly either.

Once we got to the hospital, things began to get less panicky. I got examined by various doctors, male and female, young and old, and I was so keen for them to sort me out I wasn't even embarrassed. My parents turned up. Dad went bonkers, but at the same time he was gloating – like getting your balls stamped on was the inevitable conclusion of not doing your homework. Hello? Sanity over here. Earth to madman. Do you read me?

They told me it was just bruising – bad bruising, but nothing worse than that. Then they decided to keep me in overnight for observation. Just in case.

'Just in case of what?' I asked. The nurse muttered something about it being an important area. You can say that again.

Billie Trevors. Just my luck. If I'd have known it was her, I wouldn't have gone anywhere near her. She ought to have a sign tattooed on her forehead – PSYCHOPATH. Mum and Dad were practically falling over themselves in their desire to get her locked up forever, but when Hannah and Jim came over to see me after school was out, they weren't nearly so keen. Actually – unbelievably – I could see Mum weakening at one point, when Hannah started going on about all the personal problems she had to overcome, but Dad and I were unmoved. It was the first time in ages I'd agreed with the old man. It made a nice change.

By the time everyone had gone home and they'd fed us our slops, it was getting late. Things down there felt a bit better by then, but I hadn't had a chance to have a proper look – practically everyone else in the ward had had a close-up of my manhood except me. I kept feeling them – they felt enormous and hot. The left one felt really weird, like it belonged to someone else. It was scary. I kept giving it a little nudge, seeing how it was getting on, until one of the nurses came along, sat on the edge of the bed and had a little word.

'Chris,' she said. 'I know you've had a testicular injury, and you know you've had a testicular injury. But to everyone else in the ward, it just looks like you're playing with yourself. OK?'

'Oh. God. Right.'

'My advice is leave it alone. Try not to worry. You'll just make it flare up. OK?'

'Right. Sorry. OK.'

Shame, shame, shame! Caught fiddling in public! The most embarrassing thing that can ever happen to you. I couldn't even check my wounds without everyone thinking I was some sort of hospital perv. 'Try not to worry,' she says. I was bound to worry, wasn't I? The words she used . . . *testicular injury* . . . *testicular injury* . . . *testicular injury* . . . kept swirling round my head. In the end I had to go to the loo to have a proper look and, man, they were quite a sight. It was the left one. It was enormous. It looked very painful to me. It was. I sat there on the loo, looking at it and giving it a prod. Ouch.

'Leave it till tomorrow,' she'd said.

Yeah, right. Problem with that. I had to know if it still worked. Oh, I know, they have all their little tests and examinations and so on, but, ultimately, there's only one test that really counts. You know what I mean. The proof of the pudding. Experience is the best scientist. That sort of thing.

I needed to know. Without going into too much

detail, it involved a longer-than-usual trip to the toilet. It was a tricky job – it was a delicate juggling act, if you get my meaning. But it worked. I went back to bed a relieved man.

That night it started hurting reeeeeeeeeeeal bad.

Rob

I ran out of the Brant and off down the road. It was a nightmare. It was my life. It was never going to stop.

'I'm sorry, Billie, I'm sorry, I'm sorry, I'm sorry,' I shouted, even though there was no one there to hear. I think I was crying. I'd pulled down Billie Trevors's kecks in public. Everyone saw. I was dead. I was going to get beaten up and have my nuts trampled on forever and ever. And then I was dead.

I ran and ran, and then suddenly there was this awful blare, this howling roaring noise right next to me. I froze to the spot, waiting for the crunch. Then I turned my head . . . and there was this huge lorry just a few metres away coming right at me.

And – I paused. Yeah. I stood there and watched it and I thought, *I could just stand here and it'd smack into me and that'd be that*. Because, you know what? That'd be all right, really. In fact, it'd be a good deal better than what was going to happen to me if I got out the way.

And there'd be blood and guts. How metal is that? Yeah! I'd have died in my Metallica T-shirt!

I jumped back and the lorry went past, horn blaring, the bloke shouting something at me. I got on to the other kerb, but I was really shaken up, because I nearly had just stood there. I'd been less than a second away from death. It would have been so easy to let it go over me.

I'd wanted to die.

Get a grip, will you, Robbie, mate, I said to myself. *You don't die in a road accident because it gives your T-shirt better cred.*

My life wasn't making sense any more.

I was at the bus stop before I realized I had nowhere to go except home. And why would I want to go there? That's where Philip was, sitting on his arse drinking beer and watching daytime TV or whatever he does to get through his nasty, pointy little day.

I sat down on a bench. I pulled off the top Jim had lent me and turned the T-shirt the right way round, to see if it had suffered any more, but it didn't look any different. Billie had done most of the damage with her feet. I was a mass of new bruises. I felt them all over to see if bruises from Billie were different from the other ones that lesser beings dealt out. I reckon they were a bit sharper when you pressed them with your fingers, maybe, but I guess a bruise is a bruise, even when it's been dealt out by the queen of pain.

You have to hand it to her, though. I've been beaten

up before – I'm an expert at it – but Billie has style. I hadn't even seen most of the blows she landed. The others, thugs like Martin Riley, they're just hammers on legs. Billie was an artist. It was a privilege to be beaten up by her . . . Only, it was the sort of privilege you could do without.

I pulled out the T-shirt and gazed at it in awe. It was a mess. The skeleton looked half dead. His head was hanging off on one side, the bike was ripped in the middle. He was so creased he'd started to crumble. The whole thing was stained, ripped and mangled.

It was the most metal thing I ever saw.

'You and me have got a lot in common, mate,' I told it. 'Look at us! We've been beaten up, abused, kicked, spat on, shat on . . . and here we are, both still standing, ready for more.'

The skeleton waved his hands in the air and laughed. 'Yeah, man! This is the life. When are the drugs and the women and trashing hotel rooms going to start?' he said, and we both fell around laughing, because to get those kind of things you have to be in a band. And to be in a band you have to have an instrument.

You know – I could have been good. I really knew how to beat out a metal rhythm. Back in Manchester, me and my mate Frankie, we were really getting it together for a while. Frankie was a couple of years older than me, but we lived on the same street. I used to go round to his place to play on his PlayStation and he used to come round to mine with his guitar. He only had an old acoustic, but he used to thrash the hell out of it and I used to thrash the hell out of the drums. We couldn't play all that well, but man! – We made a *noise*. It was the best time of my life, playing death metal with Frankie. We were on the same wavelength. Liked the same music, everything. Slipknot, Metallica, Slaughter. He used to write lyrics – really cool lyrics. We had our own songs. We were going to be a band. We even had a name for it: Kill All Enemies. It was this game we used to play on the PlayStation, a shoot-'em-up, and when you began each mission, that's what used to flash up on the screen: Kill All Enemies. Somehow, it summed up our lives. That's how it felt anyhow. Frankie had a step-dad too, see. We both hated our stepdads. We used to sit for hours, playing games and thinking of new and worse names to call them.

Then he moved. Must have only been a year or so ago. It was soon after that when Philip took my drums away. My nan gave me those drums. He didn't do it while she was still around – he's too much of a coward for that. But, as soon as she was dead, he was in my room taking them down. Flogged 'em. I didn't even get the money for them. He said he'd give it to me when he got some more, but he never did. He spent it on beer. Sold my dreams for a few more cans for him and his mates.

'I wonder what he's going to do when he finds out we're kicked out the Brant,' I said.

'Sod him, man. Let's play,' said Skelly. I hit the drums. I could hear Slipknot in my head, 'Dead Memories', one of my favourite tracks. I was onstage, pounding the skins, driving out the devil, beating a path out of hell. Skelly whacked a riff on the electric guitar and the crowd went mad. Then both of us burst into song at exactly the same time, our own version, singing Philip away . . .

'You bar-arse-stard. You bar-arse-stard. You bar-arse-stard,' we screamed, at the top of our voices.

An old lady sitting on a nearby bench got up and walked away. We waved at her. You can't expect someone over a hundred to like Slipknot – be fair. Skelly scratched his bony skull.

'Do you think she knows something we don't?' he said, and he tried to wink. 'Know what I mean?' he said.

'Yeah, I see what you mean,' I said. I was sitting there playing the imaginary drums, talking out loud to a skeleton. Worse, to a picture of a skeleton. I didn't care. I wiped my nose on my arm and smiled at the other people on the benches around us. Most of them were already moving off.

Me and Skelly, we had a bit of a chat and sorted a few things out on the bus on the way home. We decided that I needed to be very careful. We decided I was in the process of going stark raving bonkers.

I got back. He was in. He's always in. Telly on loud, which was a blessing, because at least I managed to get upstairs without him noticing. I put the headphones on and lay down in the bed.

And . . . ahhh. The Philip world disappears.

I push my fingers into my eyes . . .
It's the only thing that slowly stops the ache . . .
But it's made of all the things I have to take . . .
Jesus, it never ends, it works its way inside . . .
If the pain goes on . . .
Aaaaaaaah!

Yeah, man. Say it for me.

Philip went out at lunchtime – down the pub, I expect. I crept downstairs for a few minutes to raid the fridge. Davey came home about three. Philip was still out. The phone rang. I left it, but it rang again. It was probably the Brant.

I went down to check. Three messages. First one, never guess. It's me mam.

I got it up. 'Phil,' she says. She wants him, not me and Davey. Him. 'Phil, I've gone for good this time. I don't want you looking for me so I'm not saying where I am. I'm sorry you're on your own with the boys for now, but it won't be long. I'll get it sorted. It's fair. Davey's yours and Robbie – I know he thinks of you as his real dad – he's known you since he was ten. I'm sorry . . . I'm really sorry, but we both knew it was going to happen.'

There was a pause. I could hear muffled voices, like she was talking to someone at the other end. Then, behind me the lounge door opened and there was Philip. He's like a ghost – I hadn't heard a thing. How can I be so stupid?

‘I’m trusting you. I’m trusting you,’ said Mum’s voice. There was another pause. ‘You knew it was going to happen,’ she said. Then she put the phone down. I turned off the answerphone.

‘You nosey little bastard.’

‘No.’

‘What had that to do with you?’

‘I was checking for messages.’

‘You never get any messages on that – you have your phone.’

‘I do get some. I’m out of credit.’

‘You’re always out of credit. You can’t keep your snotty nose out, can you?’ He came right up, right up close. In my face. Then the lounge door opened again and Davey came out into the hall. He does that because he knows it won’t be so bad if he’s there.

‘Dad,’ he said.

‘Shut up,’ said Philip. He leaned across me and pressed the buttons so another message came up.

‘Mr Mansfield, it’s about your son, Robert. There was an incident at Brant Pupil Referral Unit earlier today. Robert ran off and we haven’t seen him since. We need to discuss the matter with you urgently. Could you ring us back, please, on . . .’

He turned it off. ‘You couldn’t even keep that together, could you?’

‘It wasn’t my fault!’

‘You pulled down some girl’s trousers and it’s not your fault? You dirty little git.’

‘No.’

'That bloody T-shirt,' he said, as if the T-shirt explained to him why I went around pulling girls' trousers down.

'Dad,' said Davey. 'Dad, don't . . .'

'You go to your room.'

'Dad.'

'Get up!' he bawled suddenly, and Davey climbed the stairs, not looking at me. That's when I knew it was going to be bad, when he sent Davey upstairs. If he doesn't want him to see.

We waited until Davey was in his room because it's no sight for a kid. Then I made a dash for the door, but I had no chance – he was only a few steps away. I fumbled with the latch and he had me by the collar and marched me into the living room and pushed me to the floor. Well, he didn't push me, I just went down. And then *bang bang bang* with the foot. He bent down a couple of times to punch me. It was even worse than Billie. I mean, she really knows how to do the do, but somehow it's still worse when it's your dad doing it. Even if he's really only your stepdad.

Bang bam bam bam. Neither of us ever say anything. I go into a kind of dream. One bit of me's squirming and yelling, the other bit's just watching, wondering what's going on. I kept thinking about my mum. Does she really think I think of him as my dad? That's what was going through my head. Does she really think that?

Billie

Hannah kept calling. I didn't answer. She left messages – 'Billie, I need to talk to you. Billie, don't do anything stupid. Billie, please ring.'

They were ringing for an ambulance when I left. All he was trying to do was stop me, and I put him in hospital. That's me, that's what I am. A nutter. It's assault now. I'm not even looking at the LOK. I'm looking at Secure.

You know what? I'm not doing time for anyone.

I do care, Billie. I'll be there for you, Billie. Billie Billie Billie. Yeah, where are you going to be, Hannah – in the Secure Unit? Will you really? I don't think so.

I turned the phone off.

I was on my own now. I went round to Star Burgers to see if Cookie was there.

I came round the back and pushed open the kitchen door. You should have seen his face – he never knows whether to look pleased or cross when I show up at work. I've been seeing him on and off since I was fourteen. He likes it how young I am. 'Jail bait,' he says. He's twenty-five and he likes having a young girl, but he doesn't like me hanging around with his mates at work because he's scared of getting done. He shows me off to his mates at home, though. He has this friend, Jez, he hangs around with. They do everything together. Once, Cookie even tried to get me to give it a go with Jez – can you believe the nerve of that?

'Why would I want to do that? He's minging.'

'Why not? It won't hurt. He never gets a shag.'

'No, Cookie. Bloody hell.' He hasn't got a clue. 'Wouldn't you be jealous?'

'No.'

'You're an idiot. Why do you think he never gets a shag?'

'Why?'

'Because he's minging!'

'So? I'm minging. We're all minging. None of us are exactly page three, are we, Billie?'

'Speak for yourself.'

I didn't go round there for ages after that. He never raised it again so I guess he got the message. I don't know what he sees in Jez anyhow. He does everything Jez says. If Jez wants a beer, they drink beer. If Jez wants voddie, they drink voddie. If Jez wants a burger, Cookie says, 'They're in the freezer, mate.' Then he goes and does it for him.

It was lunchtime, and he was that busy he didn't have time to come out and talk. He gave me a tenner, though, and smuggled a burger out to me before he went back in.

'I'm on lates tonight. Could see you later in the week, eh?' he said. 'Me and Jez, getting some beers in. Fancy it?'

That was Cookie's idea of a good night out – beers with Jez, some weed, then half a bottle of voddie to wash it down. They really know how to drink, those two. I always get out of it dead quick, but sometimes you need to get off your face – like today, for instance. This might be my last few days of freedom.

I ate the burger and bought a magazine and a packet of ciggies with the money. I managed to nick a can of lager from the Spar along the road. I went to Statside and hid by the lock-ups, where I used to hang out with Jane and Sue. I read my mag and smoked my fags. I kept thinking about that kid I stamped on. All he was doing was trying to help his mate, and look what he got.

Later on, Jane and Sue turned up and we talked about the fight – the Battle of Betty, they were calling it. It'd made the papers. Apparently it'd even been in some of the nationals. They were dead chuffed. We went over it like you do – what I did, what they did, what the enemy did, how bad we did them over.

It was kinda fun but . . . not how it used to be. Fighting used to be my life. I'm not saying I don't enjoy it any more, but it's a lot harder, once you start thinking about the kids you stamped on for no reason. If I'm honest, though, it's not even them I feel sorry for – it's me. That's pathetic, isn't it? It was Hannah made me think like that, getting inside my head during personal-development sessions at the Brant. I went in there thinking I was the hardest thing on two legs and I came out just wanting to cry all the time. Personal development? Personal bloody tragedy. Once you realize that all you're doing is digging a deeper and deeper hole for yourself it takes the fun out of it.

But the thing is, after that, you're supposed to get better. You're supposed to realize who you are and what you want and where you're going and take control and be responsible and make something of yourself. And – I haven't. Two years later and I'm worse off now than when I first met her. I don't like my old mates; I can't make new mates. I don't like fighting any more. I don't like anything.

She thought she was giving me something, but in the end she was just taking it away.

Sue let me kip on her floor that night, smuggled me in through her window after she went to bed. She wasn't very happy about it. The next day, I hung around, copped another burger off Cookie. I wasn't ready to go back and face the music. I was going down. I thought, *I might as well sneak a few more days in while I have the time.*

And – I had some business to sort out.

Katie. Doing all the housework and looking after Sam while that cow lies in her bed, drunk. In another year or so it'll be Katie sitting out in the park, drinking beer and waiting to get locked up. And what was I doing about it? Stamping on some poor stupid kid's nuts for no reason, when I ought to be sorting out that bloke Mum's got round there, helping her booze away the child support.

That's me all over – always doing the right things to the wrong people. I felt bad about that lad. How could I go round and tell my mum how to behave while I had that on my conscience?

I needed to put my own house in order. I might be a lot of things, but I'm not a hypocrite. I needed to tell him. I needed to say I'm sorry, I shouldn't have done it. I lost it. After that I could go round and hide out a few days at Cookie's, get myself together. Then, when I was feeling more myself, I could go round and sort my mum out.

And after that . . . after that they could do what they liked to me.

I drank a couple more cans in the park, then I felt ready. I stubbed out my fag and got up. I'd start with the easy one first. See how I got on with that. Then my mum.

Chris

The police came round the next day to take a statement about the attack. I don't know what they wanted a statement from me for. Mad Billie had done it in front of everyone. Jim, Hannah, all the kids in the PRU – they'd all seen it. They had enough witnesses to lock her up and throw the key away forever, as far as I could make out. Sounded like a good idea.

When they'd done, the coppers closed their books and stood to go.

'We've been after her for a long time,' one of them said.

'What'll happen to her?' I asked. I was feeling a bit bad, actually. I may have laid it on a bit thick in that statement, looking back. You can't blame me. Not only was I stuck in hospital with a nasty testicular injury, I'd also been tortured with embarrassment by nurses.

'She'll get locked up if they've got any sense,' said the copper.

'Where is she now? Have you arrested her?'

'No, she's on the run.'

'She's run off? Where to?'

'Well, if we knew that we'd be round taking her in. She'll turn up. She hasn't got anywhere to go. She knows it's over for her now. She's just putting off the day of judgement. There isn't a judge in the country won't chuck the book at her.'

'She's got away with murder in the past,' the other copper said.

'How come?'

'They don't like locking kids up, even kids like Billie Trevors. And she has friends. Those people in the Brant don't want her put away. They always think they can sort them out. But kids like Billie Trevors don't learn. The only thing you can do with her is lock her up.'

It made me feel better about laying it on a bit thick. If she was going to be let off lightly, I needed to redress the balance. I made up my mind: if it ever got to court, I'd lay it on as thick as I could, get her locked up for as long as humanly possible. I mean, she's clearly a monster. A ball crusher.

I felt better then.

Alex came to see me after school that day. I was pleased to start off with. I was getting fed up with him lately, but it gets so boring in hospital I'd have been happy to see Genghis Khan.

I was the talk of the school, apparently. The boy who got his nads flattened by Billie Trevors was all everyone could talk about. According to Alex, the teachers were loving it in a 'that's what happens when you get into trouble' kind of way. Just like my dad.

'What, if you get excluded, you're going to get your balls flattened? How pathetic!' I exclaimed.

'Yes, but they have a point, don't they?' said Alex. 'It's the sort of people who go there. The sort of people who get excluded.'

Pure blind prejudice – and there's the teachers encouraging it. Unbelievable. And these people call themselves educators. I was *so* irritated at them making hay out of my misfortune like that.

'I think I felt better before you came here,' I told Alex.

'I can go if you like,' he said. But I let him stay, which was a mistake because he spent the entire time nagging me to let him take a picture of my nads on his phone.

'No! Are you mad? Why would I let you do that?'

'Everyone's curious.'

'Who?'

'Everyone. All the lads – and the girls.'

'Which girls?'

'Beverley Summers.'

I used to go out with Beverley. Sort of.

'Maybe she wants to compare them. Before and after,' sniggered Alex. That was his idea of humour. And then before I had a chance to respond – guess what? I mean, guess who? Only the nut-stamping lunatic herself, Billie Trevors. How psycho is that? I spotted her at once, as soon as the door opened. She had a face like thunder, glaring about, scowling, peering into the beds. Talk about ugly. She looked like someone had peed in her shoes.

She'd come to finish off the job.

'Alex . . . Alex . . . !' I hissed.

'What?'

'It's her – that girl . . .'

'What girl?'

'Billie Trevors. The one who stamped on my bollocks. She's coming this way!'

'Where?'

'Over there. She's come to finish the job . . . I interfered in her fight . . . Call the nurse . . . Alex? Alex!'

Because Alex, dear Alex, my best mate, had shot off to hide down the ward.

'Alex! Come back! I'll never forgive you for this . . . Alex!'

It was too late. Psychonut was already upon me.

'Hi,' I said brightly, while my hand groped desperately for the bell to call the nurse.

Billie stood there glaring down at me. She was in a right state – hair all over the place, clothes creased, stains down her front.

'I've been feeling bad,' she said.

My mouth opened. Nothing came out.

She glanced at the bed. 'Mind if I sit down?'

'. . . Go ahead.'

Billie sat down and clenched her hands together. Her fingernails were black.

'How are you?' she said.

'A bit, you know, sore.'

'I didn't mean it.'

'Didn't you?'

'I lost it.' She sat there chewing her lip. She seemed calm but I was worrying about mood swings. What were the signs? How long did it take her to go from calm to monster?

'Nothing permanent, then?'

'No! I can still . . . have children and everything. They just, you know, kept me in for observation.'

Billie looked up at the ceiling and smiled.

'Thank God for that. I was really worried. I know you were just jumping in to save your mate – it wasn't anything to do with you. And he just . . .'

'Grabbed out at the wrong thing,' I suggested.

Billie blushed. 'Yeah. If I'd have known, I'd have changed me pants.'

And we both laughed.

Funny, eh? One minute you're doing your best to get her locked up, the next you're sitting there having a laugh with her. I told her what really happened. That big bully kid, Roly Poly, it wasn't his fault. He was tripped. I saw it. It was Ed – the most irritating kid in the world.

I don't know why I told her that. Roly had it coming. You heard what he said while I was writhing on the floor in mortal agony? 'I still owe you.' I still owe you – after I'd had my balls crushed trying to save his sorry fat hide. I should have kept my mouth shut and let Billie destroy him in her own time – but it wasn't fair. As for Ed – that's another matter. I had some business with Ed, and maybe Roly Poly did as well. And maybe telling Billie about it was sorting it out on both our accounts.

We had a good old chat in the end, me and Billie. When she's not scowling, Billie actually . . . she could be pretty hot if she dressed herself right. And sweet. Amazingly – but yeah. You can read everything that's going on with her. When I told her about Ed, you should have seen her. First she looked amazed, then she looked furious, then she looked really sad.

'He was tripped. And I battered him. And then I battered you.'

'It's not your fault. He pulled your trousers down. He deserved it.'

'No, he didn't. I just went crazy. Anyway, I just came in to say I'm really sorry.'

'Sorry accepted,' I said.

She stood up to go. 'That's what I came to say,' she said. 'I'll go now.'

'Er . . . you wanna grape or something? Biscuit?' I asked. Now that she'd come to say sorry, I didn't want to let her go. It was stupid, really – she was a known psychopath, unable to control her violence by her own admission. But I liked her. At least she wasn't bland. At least she wasn't hiding up the ward thinking about herself like Alex.

Billie glanced around her, scowling away, like it might not be safe. She looked like one of those Manga comics when she scowled like that. Then she eyed the food. 'Thanks,' she muttered gruffly, and sat back down and started wolfing down the fruit and biscuits and stuff on the plate beside me like a dog.

'. . . Hungry,' she said when she saw me looking.

'Yeah. What have you been doing, then?' I asked her.

'On the run,' she said, and she gave me a bit of a smile. 'Desperado,' she said with her mouth full. 'Outlaw.'

'Yeah, the police said.'

'The cops? They've been round here?' she said, pausing and looking around.

'Yeah, yeah – hours ago. They wanted a . . .' Then I remembered what I'd said to them and changed the subject. 'But what's it really like?' I said.

'What?'

'On the run. I mean, it sounds like fun, but is it?'

Billie pulled a face. 'It's crap,' she said. 'I haven't been home since.' She ducked her head. 'I'm in such shit.'

'What'll they do when they get you? The police, I mean?'

'Dunno yet. Secure, in the end. The LOK for now.'

'What's that?'

'That's where they send all the bad kids.'

'I thought that was the Brant.'

'The Brant is for beginners. The LOK is a proper concentration camp.'

I felt dreadful.

'Won't they let you back in the Brant until then?'

Billie shook her head. 'That was my last chance. I messed up big time. They really put their necks out for me and I let everyone down. Why would they give me another chance? I wouldn't.'

She couldn't look at me. Her eyes had gone red. I looked away and picked myself a grape, and she wiped her eyes on the back of her hand. Big hard Billie – and here she was, sitting at the edge of my bed trying not to cry.

'I can't help myself,' she said in a gruff voice. I wanted to hold her hand or pat her on the shoulder or something, but I was too scared.

We chatted a bit. Talked about music and films. She liked really ordinary things – the same sort of things I liked. Keanu Reeves, Bruce Willis, Angelina Jolie. I suppose I was expecting her to like something really strange. Music was the same – rap, rock . . . and heavy metal, which seemed to fit more.

'Metal, yeah,' she said. 'Wanna hear my death growl?'

'What's that? Yeah – go on.'

She did this voice – it was hilarious. Like a bear with a sore throat, only singing. And the amazing thing was it was in tune. It was so loud and deep it made me laugh my head off. She was laughing too, snorting biscuits over the bed. Then there was a kerfuffle down the end of the ward. Billie stood up and looked over.

Over by the desk, on the other side of the double doors, there was a flash of dark blue. A uniform. A face looked through the glass panel.

Police.

'It wasn't me, Billie, I didn't call them.'

Billie looked down at me with a face full of scorn.

'No one ever does,' she said. She tipped back her head, and walked off towards the double doors.

'Billie, don't go!' I shouted. 'Do a runner!'

But it was too late. She pushed open the door at the end of the ward. I wondered if she was going to put up a fight, but she didn't. She just walked through without a glance back and the police closed in on her on the other side, quick, like they were catching something. They were. She looked back then, over her shoulder at me, her white face, scared like a little kid.

Then she was gone.

A couple of minutes later Alex came up, grinning all over his stupid face.

'I saved your nads,' he said.

'How come,' I said, 'you manage to cock up everything you ever do?'

Hannah

I got a call off Barbara Barking at eight.

'They've picked her up. She was at the hospital, getting back on to that boy she stamped on.'

Billie – no!

'Where are you?'

'At home. They're going to give me a ring when I can go and pick her up.'

'You get down there right away. Tell them you want to see her *now*.'

'But they said it could be hours yet.'

'We don't have to do it their way. Get down there, give her a bit of support, even if they don't tell her now she'll know later on you were there for her. I've got to finish up here. I'll come and join you soon as I've sorted out some care for my Joe.'

I rushed around like a maniac getting things sorted. By the time I arrived, Barbara and Dan were sitting holding hands in the waiting room, every inch the concerned parents. I had a quick pow-wow – Billie had already been in there two hours. Her social worker had been and gone and she was still locked up. They had her just where they wanted her. As luck would have it they had Sergeant Farrell on the desk. We're old mates, me and Sergeant Farrell. I told him a while ago.

'Think you know it all, don't you, Sergeant? Maybe you do. But so do I. So while I'm here – do it by the book, right?'

No point in being coy when it comes to people like that.

'I'm here to see Billie Trevors,' I told him.

Farrell hardly looked up from his paperwork.

'She's being questioned at the moment,' he said.

'Has she had her phone call?'

'I'm not aware . . .'

'Then I'll do it for her, shall I? She's still a minor. If you don't mind.' And I straightened up as if I was expecting to get taken through.

'I'll have a word when I've finished filling in this form,' he told me, without looking up.

'You have a vulnerable child locked up in there. I want to see her now.'

He looked at me as if I was made out of sick. 'Vulnerable?' he said. 'Do you know what she did?'

'She kicked a bloke in the balls. Don't tell me you haven't done the same thing. I don't see you being held in the cells overnight.'

He looked away and shook his head disgustedly.

I leaned across the desk. 'I'm having lunch with your chief constable next week, Sergeant. Let's hope your name comes up in a positive light, shall we?'

'I don't see much chance of that happening if it's you saying it,' he told me.

'If you stick to doing your job rather than harassing prisoners you don't personally like, your name *will* come up in a positive way. Now, I'd like to know what's going on here, please. Has she been arrested? On what grounds are you holding her?'

'She's helping us with our enquiries,' he said calmly, going all formal on me. 'Take a seat, Mrs Holloway. We'll let you know when we're ready for you.'

I stayed where I was. I waited. He waited.

'I'm waiting,' I said.

He put down his pen and went out round the back to have a word with his inspector.

I shouldn't do it really. I expect he just went back to the cells and gave her a hard time. But Billie would want me to give them some stick.

In between nagging the police, I had a catch-up with Barbara and Dan. I hadn't had much to do with them before, but over the past couple of days we'd been on the phone all the time. She's not exactly what you'd call stable. It's all sunshine and light one minute, fits of rage the next. Today, it was the guilt. 'Oh, Hannah, it's all my fault, I've been too strict, I called the police, I've not given her a fair chance.'

'Yes, Barbara,' I replied. 'It *is* all your fault. You called an armed-response unit out because she lost it after going to give her mum a birthday present – despite the fact that you've been told by several sources, including myself, many times, when her mum's birthday is and to expect problems around that time. You chose that evening to try and ground her for a month. Well done.'

Only I didn't.

'No, Barbara, you mustn't blame yourself, don't be daft . . . *blah blah blah*.'

It's her husband, Dan, has the level head. I'd like to say to her, *Can you not listen to your husband, love? He's got more sense in his little finger than you have in your entire body.* But she's the dominant one. She doesn't just wear the trousers, she's got his Y-fronts on as well. He knows it's wrong, the way she goes on, but he hasn't got the guts to put his foot down and say no.

That's life. No one gets a degree in bringing up kids – you get what you're given. At least she sticks with Billie, which is more than her other carers have done. And that counts for a lot.

I got a bit more of the picture sitting in the waiting room that night, in between chasing up the police. Billie hadn't told me the half of it. I knew that she'd punched him, for example; I didn't know how many times. Or about the time she punched her. Bloody hell. By the time I'd heard it all I'd changed my mind a little bit. They certainly had sticking power.

It was a puzzle, for sure. Why hang on to a kid that you're unsuited to care for, even after she's punched your lights out two or three times? Not that I'm one to talk, mind. Why do any of us do it? Me, I have my work at the Brant, I have my son, Joe – that's my life. I don't have time for anything else. I don't see anyone, I don't go out. I haven't had a bloke for years, and that was an affair with a married man – it's all I have time for. It's my job to do everything in my power to be the best mother I can to those kids. It's a hard job – it's impossible, actually. The pay's rubbish. Why do I do it? I don't know. But I do it and I love it and I wouldn't have it any other way.

But Barbara – calling the armed-response team in? Her and her husband getting black eyes once a month? What does she get out of it?

'You're a professional, Hannah,' she said. 'You have a lot of experience with girls like Billie.'

'There's not many quite like Billie, but yeah.'

'When we first took her on, they said how if you're just prepared to see it through, a child will learn to love you. Tell me honestly: do you think Billie will ever come to see me as a mother?'

I thought, *Oh, gawd. Is that it? She wants to be Billie's mum.*

You'd think it'd work, wouldn't you? She wants to be a mum and Billie wants a mum – it should be a match made in heaven. Except . . .

'Billie already has a mum, Barbara. She's a crap mum, but she's still her mum and no one's ever going to take her place.'

Barbara stiffened up. What else could I say? You should never take on a teenage foster-child because you want to be their mother. It isn't going to happen.

I touched her on the knee.

'I'm sorry.'

She nodded stiffly. Ah, bless. We all want someone to love, and we all want someone to love us back.

'Do you still want her to come back to you?' I asked.

She didn't hesitate, give her that. 'I still want her,' she said. 'She might not be able to love me, but I can still love her, can't I?' And Dan, sitting next to her, suddenly beamed like an angel.

'That's my girl,' he said. 'Of course we have to keep her.'

Shut me up, someone, will you? I've been doing this for twenty years, and what do I know? Unsuitable they may be – well, anyone suitable would have dumped Billie ages ago. I leaned across and gave her a big hug. 'You can't ever be her mum, Barbara, but I never said she won't learn to love you.'

What is it about that girl? How come we all keep on coming back to her, despite everything she does? She's violent, unpredictable; she's dangerous. And you just can't help loving her.

They let her out about an hour later, after a lot of noise on my part. She'd been arrested for actual bodily harm but not charged. She would be, though. The best we could hope for was to get it down to assault. She looked ruined. Red eyes, grey skin. They hadn't beaten her and they hadn't starved her or tortured her in any way. What they had done, they'd locked up a vulnerable girl in a bare cell on her own for three hours when she was distressed. Isn't that enough?

At least we had a nice little welcoming committee

there waiting for her when she got out. We all went over to give her a hug, Barbara first. Then I got my turn. I hugged her tight. 'You're doing great,' I whispered in her ear. She wasn't looking at anyone, no eye contact. Not good. We all filed out. The police were still on her. One of the young coppers smiled at her and opened the door like he was being nice.

'See you next time, Billie,' he said.

I was just waiting for someone to step out of line. I pounced.

'What do you mean by that, saying that to a child? Don't tell me that's part of your training, because I know it's not.'

The copper opened his mouth to bleat.

'I'll have your name and number, I think,' I said, and whipped out me pen. 'I have a meeting with your chief constable next week. I can bring it up then. Telling a child she has no future . . .'

'I didn't mean it like that.'

'That's for your superiors to decide. I've known children in worse trouble than our Billie turn things round and come out with more of a future than you'll ever have. Name?' I snapped. I took down the poor guy's name and number and we all marched out, heads in the air, into the car park, like it was them who was in trouble, not Billie. As soon as we got outside, I started to cackle.

'Did you see his face? Oh my God!' I chortled. 'He bit off more than he bargained for there.'

I thought we'd all have a laugh about it – not. Dan

gave an embarrassed little smile. Barbara gave the slightest of snorts down her nose, like, *We don't have time for this*. Billie was just too far gone to notice, I think.

'Well,' I said to her. 'I told you I'd be here for you.'

Barbara led her to the car, and I followed on behind. Billie dodged down and got straight in. Still no eye contact. Barbara and Dan followed. I paused, and bent down to the window.

'Barbara. Can I come? Do you mind?'

She looked at me and glanced at Billie in the back, and for a moment I thought she was going to say no. I wouldn't have blamed her – it was the Barbara and Billie show now. She had the hard job. I just popped in and out. But she nodded and I opened the door and got in the back beside Billie. We drove along in silence for a good while before she spoke.

'What's going to happen to me?' she said.

I gave it to her straight – she may as well start getting used to it.

'You're going to get done this time, Billie. That boy you got, his parents are going to press charges.'

'I went to say sorry,' she said.

'Ah, did you? Ah, love. But sorry isn't enough.'

'Nothing's ever enough,' she said. 'I wouldn't have been caught if I hadn't gone in.'

'Yes, you would, Billie. You know you would.'

'He shopped me, that kid. I went to say sorry and he shopped me.'

'Do you blame him?'

'I'll have him for that . . .'

'Billie, stop it! This situation is your doing and you know it.'

There was a long pause. 'What do you think I'm going to get?' she asked.

'I don't know, Billie. A few months, I expect.'

She looked desperate, poor love. I felt so sorry for her. Billie needs helping, not punishing. Don't get me wrong. I understand that people are going to get put away sometimes. But why does it have to be in a place that makes them worse, not better?

'I don't think I can do that,' she said.

'We're going to fight it,' said Barbara, leaning across from the front. 'Don't you worry, Billie. We're going to fight it.'

'Too right we are,' I said. But I knew, and I think Billie knew – they had her this time. We could appeal till we were blue in the face. Because you know what? She deserved it. I didn't even know in all conscience whether I could argue for letting her off any more.

I looked at her and I thought how hard she'd tried, how hard we'd all tried to get her life together. And I thought, *You know what, Billie? I thought you were going to make it, I really did. But now – I just don't know.*

She was going down fast, and I hadn't got a trick left to stop her.

Chris

'The good news is,' said my dad, 'you don't have to go back to the Brant.'

'A bit of a relief all round,' said my mum. They looked at each other and smiled. Obviously getting me away from the Brant was a major personal triumph for them. 'The school thinks you've been through enough. You can go back in as soon as you're ready.'

I closed my eyes and sighed. The thought of school – it just made my heart sink. Yes, I know, I got my bollocks stamped at the Brant, but that was bad luck. I'd been liking it up to that point. It was only half of one morning, but at least they treated you like a human being. It wasn't sir this and miss that. It wasn't boring me to death. The other kids liked it. So did I.

And, anyway, I'd made friends with Billie. No one was going to dare even touch me now.

'Billie Trevors has been arrested for ABH – Actual Bodily Harm,' said my dad. 'That's the other good news.'

'That's not fair,' I said.

They stopped smiling and looked curiously at me.

'Pardon?'

'I think we should drop the charges,' I said.

'I don't believe I'm hearing this,' muttered my dad.

'You could have been seriously injured. You know that, don't you?' said Mum.

It all seemed pretty straightforward to me. Billie had come in to say she was sorry and she got nobbled by the rozzers because of it. It took some courage to do that. She didn't have to. And, be fair, if someone pulled down your kecks in public, you'd be cross. I was stupid to jump in, that's all.

You know what they say in a fight? Go for the biggest bugger first. In our family, that's Mum. It's like monkeys – there's always a dominant one. Dad does a lot of hooting and branch-shaking to make himself look good, but it's all show. Mum doesn't need to do that. It's her overweening mental and emotional superiority that gives her the edge – but that doesn't mean to say she doesn't have a weak spot.

'They're going to lock her up if we let them arrest her,' I said. 'The Secure Unit. Prison for kids. And she came to apologize! What's the point of locking her up if she's already reformed?'

Dad glared at me furiously. That stuff about reforming people – he can't bear it. It's a big point of issue between her and him. She believes that practically anyone, even the most hardened mass-murderer, can be made into a kind and useful member of society given the right circumstances, whereas my dad, he just believes in evil bastards.

'The longer they lock her away, the better,' he snapped. Tactics, he just don't get it.

'Hang on, hang on – he has a point there. She did come in especially to apologize, even though it got her caught,' said my mum.

And that was it. They started snorting and glaring at each other. Then the pant-hooting started and they rushed upstairs to 'talk it over'. Shortly after, suppressed shouting could be heard from an upstairs bedroom.

I had my hopes, but they were soon dashed. They came down together a bit later to announce their decision. I could tell they'd come to the wrong one by the way they were glancing conspiratorially at each other and touching one another on the arms.

'It's gone too far, Chris,' Mum said. 'You're damaging your chances at school and now you're even willing to risk damaging your chances of being a father. Quite apart,' she added sternly, with a glance at my squirming father, 'from causing strains inside the family.'

I rolled my eyes. 'I got kicked in the balls,' I said. 'It happens.'

'This is the deal,' Mum went on. 'We'll drop the charges . . .' Dad couldn't help himself and started rolling his eyes and snorting like a horse. Mum glared him into silence. '. . . We agree to drop the charges so long as you promise – promise! – on your word of honour! – to go back to school and *get on with your work*. Properly.'

'We want your word,' emphasized my dad. 'Properly,' he added, just in case there was any doubt.

'Are you seriously telling me,' I said, 'that unless I agree to your blackmail, you'll go straight ahead and get Billie locked up? Effectively ruin what chances she has of getting her life back on track?' I asked them incredulously.

Mum flinched. 'It's not like that,' she began.

'Then how is it?'

No reply.

'How do you justify that? Putting someone's whole future at risk for your own personal whim?' I asked her.

It was one of the few times I can remember Mum losing her rag.

'I justify it,' she shouted, 'on the grounds that my son is behaving like a two-year-old child who won't do anything unless he gets his own way. I justify it on the grounds that I can't think of any other way of making you knuckle down and get on with your school work and make a future for yourself. Now, Chris – do we have a deal?'

'You're holding her whole future to ransom!'

'Do. We. Have. A. Deal?' she demanded through gritted teeth.

I turned my back and stamped upstairs without bothering to answer. There was silence downstairs for a while, then they came upstairs and went into the bedroom. See? Like monkeys. He gets his reward for being good. Or maybe it's her who gets rewarded. I don't want to know.

School. Even worse – work. Billie, Billie – this is asking a lot. I was going to have to think about this one.

The solution, when it came to me, was easy. As is so often the case, it involved the application of a simple lie. I went and told them that, yes, on reflection, I agreed to their terms.

And they believed me.

Rob

After Philip was finished, I went upstairs and lay on my bed for a bit. Davey poked his head round the door to see how I was, but I wasn't ready for him.

'Go away,' I said.

'No, Rob . . .' he began.

'Get lost or I'll shout at you and then he'll come back upstairs and do me again. OK?'

'Rob . . .'

'Go on, get lost,' I said.

'I just wanted to say, Mum was at the school gates today. She was asking about you.'

I sat up. 'Did you tell him?'

'No, course I didn't. She wants to see you tomorrow.'

'Right. Don't say a word, right?'

'Right.'

'Or I'll bat yer head in!' I hissed after him, just so he knew how cross I was. I got my phone and had a check.

I could have killed myself. Mum had texted me twice to let me know she'd be at the school gates, but I'd left the phone at home so I never knew. I never use it. I needed to get back to her right now, but I had no credit. I went to Davey, but of course he had no credit, either.

'I have to let her know I'll be there,' I said.

'She knows you'll be there.'

'Does she know I'm out of school?'

'Yeah . . . But she said she'll definitely be there. She said.'

'I have to text her. Go on, go down and see if Philip'll give you some credit. He will.'

'I don't want to, Rob.'

'Go on. I'd do it for you.'

He started shuffling and whining then, because he knew it was true. 'He won't give it me.'

'You can try. What's up with you? He never hits you.'

He just pulled a face at me.

'What then?'

'I don't want to.'

'Go on . . .'

So he went, but it didn't do any good. I heard Philip shouting at him and telling him to go to his room. There were some bangs. Philip chucks things around when he's taking it out on Davey, but he never hits him. Davey came back up trying not to cry.

'You all right? Sorry, I just wanted to be able to tell Mum I'd be there,' I said.

'I'm all right, I'm all right . . .'

'Listen, Davey, you won't tell Mum, will you? About Philip and me. I don't want her worrying about that.'

Davey nodded his head and went back to his room. I shouldn't have sent him down. Philip hates it when he sides with me. It's not like what I have to put up with, though, is it? He can do that for me, at least.

The next day I was in a right state, waiting. I didn't have anywhere to go so I had to stay at home with Philip keeping an eye on me. The important thing was to make sure he never found out she'd be waiting for us. If he knew that, he'd be there – you could bet your life on it.

The next most important thing was to make sure I got there. Like I said, Philip's always at home. He stays in all day sometimes. What if I never made it? What would she think then? Like I didn't care, like I didn't want to see her, like I blamed her . . .

I was fretting about it all day, but I struck lucky. He had a job interview in the afternoon. He's a painter and decorator, Philip – proper stuff. He can do posh papers, £40, £50 a roll, paint finishes and everything. Our house, it's not big and the furniture's rubbish, but the decoration's great. People always talk about it. Trouble is he gets arguing with the boss or gets drunk and then he gets sacked so he doesn't keep his jobs for long.

'I'll need a job bringing up you and Davey, now that cow's left me in the lurch,' he told me.

We had lunch together, he made us omelettes, and then he went out.

'Don't forget – you're grounded,' he told me before he went. 'If I find you've been out that door, you're for it.'

I waited till he was well off down the road before I sneaked out the back way so the neighbours wouldn't see me. It was about two by then. I had another hour and a half.

I was crapping myself, but not about Philip. What if she wasn't there? What if she thought she hadn't heard from me so she didn't bother? That sort of thing. What if Philip came back early and found me not there and came round to school to get me? Then he'd see Mum – he'd get his hands on her. Maybe I shouldn't turn up at all in case Philip got wind of it.

But of course I did turn up. And so did she.

We had a big hug, me and her and Davey, right out in front of the gates. I didn't care. I just stood there soaking her up, the smell of her, the feel of her arms round me. I know that might sound cheesy, but that's how it is with me and my mum.

We went and had a drink in a café. We weren't there long before Mum wanted to talk to me on my own.

'Go home, go to him, Davey,' she said. 'You and me had some time to usselves yesterday. I need to talk to Robbie now.'

Davey pulled a face, but he's fair; he understood.

'I'll see you again very, very soon,' she said. 'Promise.'

He didn't like it, but he did as she said. She went out with him to say goodbye in private. She always gives you some time, my mum.

When she came back, she said, 'Come on, let's get out. I need a ciggie.'

She linked arms with me and we walked around till we found a bench, then we sat down. She lit her fag, took a long drag, leaned back and said, 'So, what's going on with you, Robbie?'

'What do you mean?'

'You know what I mean. Look at you. You're a mess. You've been fighting again, haven't you? And you've been chucked out of school. How are you going to be looking out for your little brother with all this going on? You're not even at the same school as him any more.'

'School,' I told her. 'I've had enough of school. I'm always getting picked on and then getting the blame for it.'

Mum shook her head. 'You're always getting into fights, Robbie. I don't understand it. Where'd you get it from?'

I looked at her sideways. I could have told her . . . but I didn't. She has enough on her plate without me loading my troubles on her too.

I shrugged and smiled, and my mum, she smiled back.

'You're a right mess,' she laughed. 'Tell me, then. School, eh?'

So I told her – my version. I'm this bad lad and it's me that starts all the fights. Everyone thinks I'm a bit of a bully, but really I'm sticking up for the little kids. And I'm scared of no one. And then she tells me not to pick on other kids like I do, and I tell her I'd be happy to leave them be if they didn't try it on, and she tries to tell me off – but she's proud I'm so tough and know how to look after myself.

That's me. Tough boy. Yeah.

I went on and told her how super-metal that T-shirt was because it got me into trouble, like. I took off my top and showed it to her, and she could hardly believe her eyes. And I told her about Billie Trevors's kecks as well and she laughed like a drain at that, and crossed her legs and winced when I told her about that other kid's nuts.

'It should have been my nuts. But it wasn't. See? I'm a lucky kid, me,' I said.

'Funny sort of luck,' said Mum.

We sat there a while longer, and then suddenly she stood up.

'Come on,' she said.

'Where are we going?'

'My place. You're out of school, you're out the Brant. You're as well staying at mine for a few days.'

'No! You don't mean that?'

'Why not?'

See? See what I mean? My mum. She was actually taking me home with her. I was that made up, I could hardly speak. We caught the bus all the way to Manchester and we had fish and chips in town before we went back to where she was staying with a mate of hers. And . . . you have no idea. You have no idea what it felt like, sleeping somewhere where you know you're not going to get hit, knowing that someone who loves you is sleeping under the same roof. My mum. She makes everything worthwhile.

Billie

They'd done their best, I'll give them that. Cleaned it up, put up new curtains, replaced the chest of drawers I trashed. They'd even painted it. It was a pretty little room, not really my sort of thing. But they'd tried. You have to hand it to Barbara. We're totally unalike, but she does try.

I just wanted to go straight to bed, but she made me have something to eat. Hot pot, my favourite, while they sat around and watched.

'You've been doing so well,' she kept saying. It was funny, because, in a way, she was right. Things had been loads better over the past year or so. It was only this past month I was suddenly losing it. I don't know why. They kept asking me what was wrong and all I could say was . . . I don't know, I don't know, I don't know.

She said she was sorry about what she said about my mum. 'I'm just jealous of her,' she said – which was pretty honest of her. 'She's treated you so bad – I'm sorry, Billie, but you know it's true – and I try so hard to treat you well, and she gets forgiven so easily and I . . . I don't.' She shrugged. She had a point. But . . .

'It's me mum, isn't it?' I said.

'I know.'

She said sorry for calling the police as well, and that was the point when we nearly had another row. I mean, the armed-response unit?

'Billie,' said Dan, 'you have to think about how it looked to Barbara.'

'You with that huge sliver of glass in your hand, like a sword,' said Barbara.

'What did you think I was going to do with it, stab you?' I said.

'You know what you're like when you lose your rag.'

'I was over that.'

'How was Barbara supposed to know? Suppose she'd come up in the middle of it? What would have happened then?'

I was furious.

'You think that if I'd had that in my hand when I lost it I'd kill her?'

'Could you swear you wouldn't?'

'Yes! I'm not some kind of bloody psychopath.'

They looked at each other doubtfully.

'But you see how it looked.'

'I was cleaning up!'

'But you see how it *looked*, Billie.'

I went up to bed after that. I lay there staring at the ceiling. I was pleased to be home, but I wish I could have gone straight up instead of having more chat. It's the talking does my head in. And the thing is – what if they're right? Is that what I am? Some kind of nutcase who might jump up at any minute and cut their throats?

I found it so depressing that they thought that of me. It made me think – maybe all my carers thought I was like that? Dangerous. Maybe that's why they all got rid of me in the end. That's horrible. I really hope that's not true. Maybe that's what happened with the last lot, Bob and Debbie Sampson. I liked it there. They had loads of kids there, not just me. You get all this attention focused on you when you're the only one. Debbie Sampson spent most of her time with the little ones. I didn't get on with her all that well, but there was no trouble. Her husband, Bob, I got on all right with him. He was an old rocker. He was fun, Bob. He was really into his music. He had the cellar all set up like a studio – guitars and a drum kit and amps. It was even sound-proofed, sort of. We all used to go and thrash it out down there. He was well into his heavy rock, Led Zeppelin and all that kind of thing. That wasn't my scene but he had some of the real stuff too – Death and Possessed and Slayer and Arch Enemy and that. Death metal. That's when I learned how to do the death growl. He thought it was hilarious that I could do that so deep. I learned a bit of guitar too. It was great; we used to have such a good time, but then I lost it with one of the other kids. He was a bully anyway. He was picking on the little ones, only they never noticed it. They thought the sun shone out of his arse, this kid. They couldn't see what a sneaky little bastard he was. I did him over and that was it. I was out.

Trouble is – like Hannah said, what did it achieve? The bully got away with it, I got kicked out and the little kids he was bullying didn't have me there to stop him any more.

It was round about the time my mum decided to make the big split with me. There was always this idea that I could go home when things got better, but then she decided no, I was never going back. I should have known. It had been ages since she'd had me home for a weekend even.

I was in care. I got depressed. That's when Dan and Barbara offered me a place. I think they liked me when I was depressed. I was quiet, you know? I should have got depressed earlier, while I was still with the Sampsons. Maybe I'd've been able to stay there, then.

I stayed in bed late the next day. Nowhere to go, nothing to get up for. I'd have stayed there all day, but bloody Barbara kept coming up. Elevenses. Twelveses. Lunch. Oneses, twoses, she was driving me potty. She means well, Barbara, but I just wanted to be left alone. After twoses I'd had enough, so when she said she had to pop out to the shops I took my chance. I needed some money. I hadn't asked her for any, but I found a twenty in the drawer in her room. She owed me some pocket money, a tenner, I could give her back the change later. Then I left.

I went down the offie and got a few cans and took them round to drink in the park, tucked away behind the bushes where no one could see me.

I had business to attend to. *Now's as good a time as any*, I thought. Who knew how long I was going to be free to do what I wanted? I'd sorted my own house out – I'd made my peace with that lad Chris. If I'm going to go down, I'm going to go down fighting for something worthwhile. Hannah and Jim and Barbara and that, they all like to think fighting is a waste of time, but sometimes there's only one way to sort things out.

Our Katie, she's such a sweet girl, such a sweet nature. She'd do anything for you. She's like me. Not like I am now – like I was before Mum went off the rails. I couldn't stop thinking about it. And now Mum's got a new bloke. It's been ages since she had a bloke, but they're always the same. One of them had a go at me once. Back from the pub, Mum was out, he tried to get in my bed. I was only about nine. I went mad. I just started screaming, 'Get out, get out, get out!' He jumped up and stood there stinking of fags and beer.

'I were only going to read you a story, you silly mare,' he says. And he has to get in my bed to read me a bedtime story? I don't think so.

He had read me a few stories before that, give him his due. Never tried to get in my bed before, though. He went to the door and turned round and said, 'I'd never lay a hand on you, not in that way, Billie.'

Yeah, right. Well, I wasn't taking the chance.

And now she's got another one. Katie out there doing the washing. Mum nowhere to be seen, flat out with booze I expect. Bloke in the house – does what he likes. It doesn't take much working out, does it? And Katie, the way she is, she'd never tell anyone. She'd keep it all to herself to protect Mum and not rock the boat. To keep the family together. A bloke like that could do what he likes and she'd never tell. And I'm supposed to sit around and watch it? While Mum goes back on the bottle and Katie screws up her life trying to do her job for her, and some bloke nobody knows anything about comes round and does who knows what? I don't think so. I don't care if she doesn't want to see me. I'm her daughter. I'm too much trouble, am I? Is that it? Or is it because she knows I won't stand for her using Katie like another bloody servant and keeping her new bloke happy?

Who's going be there to check up on her when I'm put away? They need to know that just because I'm going down doesn't mean I'm never coming out again. And I'll tell you this, while I live and breathe, no one's going to do any harm to my little sister.

I finished off my cans, got myself a couple more and hopped on the bus. I wanted her to know I was watching her. I wanted her to know that if anything *like* what happened with me starts up again – anything, no matter how small – I was going to be right round there to sort it out. She'll have me to deal with. I wanted her to know that. I wanted them all to know that.

★

No farting about this time. I went straight there. I was going to go round the back way and get in before anyone had a chance to talk me out of it, but then I thought, *No, calm down, Billie. You don't know what's going on yet*, so I went and knocked on the door instead. Knocked – on my own front door. How do you like that?

Sam opened it.

'Sam,' I said – I was surprised. I don't know why I never thought it'd be him. 'What are you doing here? Why aren't you at school?'

'It's four o'clock,' he said.

'Is it?' I'd lost track. I peered over his shoulder. 'Is she here?' Sam looked back anxiously, but I didn't want him to be making decisions about it, so I pushed past him and went in.

It opened straight out into the front room – it didn't have a hallway. I was surprised at how small it all was. Katie was sitting in front of the TV. There was a bloke coming down the stairs. He stopped when he saw me.

'Billie,' he said.

'I'm just here to tell you – any funny business with her, with my sister, you'll have me to answer to. I'm just here to say it,' I told him.

'Billie!' Katie was on her feet, furious. 'He's done nowt! He's never done anything, Billie! Go away, Billie. Go away!' she hissed, flushing red. Embarrassed, I suppose. Well, I'd rather she be embarrassed than the other.

But I wasn't ready to go yet. 'I need to have a word with her,' I said. 'That's why I'm here.'

'She's not here, she's out . . .' began Katie. But the bloke butted in now, not that it was anything to do with him.

'You don't need to have any worries about me and Katie, Billie. There's regular visits round here from the Social and everything . . .'

'Yeah, and what do they know?'

'I'm not like that.'

'I'm not saying you are. I'm just saying.'

And then there was a movement at the top of the stairs. And her voice.

'I'll see her.'

'Muriel,' he said.

'Mum, you're not to,' said Katie.

I could see her feet, coming down. She was in her dressing gown. See? Not doing any housework in her dressing gown, is she?

'Billie,' she said. She got so far down and crouched on the stairs so I could see her face. She looked older. Wrinkles on her forehead. 'How are you, Billie? It's nice of you to come and see us.'

Nice of me! I thought, *You cow*. Down she came. She'd had her hair done. All the grey gone. She looked better. Tired though. She always looked tired.

'I want a word in private with you. You owe me that much.'

She looked at me and nodded. 'We'll go in the kitchen.'

'Mum!' Katie was furious. 'Mum, you agreed not to!'

'Agreed.' I sneered. I meant to say, *Yeah, so Katie's the responsible one, is she?* 'We'll see about that,' I said. And I thought, *This is coming out all wrong*. Because I was there to help, see? I was there to help.

Mum walked into the kitchen and I followed her, and I closed the door after me.

Just me and her.

She sat down at the table. *Bloody hell*, I thought – *it's the same table, the one we used to have when we were all together*. She'd managed to get some stuff back, then. I was supposed to sit down opposite her, but I didn't. I wasn't planning on staying long. I wasn't kidding myself. I knew I wasn't welcome. It wasn't going to be a big family reunion – I knew that.

Suddenly I was trying hard not to cry.

She smiled, but it wasn't a real smile. I got straight in.

'What's going on with Katie, then?'

'What do you mean, Billie?'

'You know what I mean. Doing the washing. What's she out there doing the washing for?'

'It's one of her chores, Billie. Everyone does chores.'

Can you believe that? Can you believe her neck?

'I had a lot of chores, didn't I?'

'That was different.'

'Was it now? Was it.'

'She has her chores. She earns her pocket money. It's right. What happened with you, Billie . . . I lost my way, but I'm trying not to make the same mistakes again, Billie, love. I'm trying. I just . . . I just don't want you to make it harder for me than it already is.'

Can you believe her? After all I did for her?

'Oh, I'm sorry!' I said. 'Am I making it hard for you? Coming round here to make sure things are all right. That's making it hard, is it? Well, fuck you.'

'No, I don't mean it like that. I'm trying to be a good mum, and . . .'

I just laughed. I just laughed at her. 'I was a better mum than you ever were,' I said, and I started crying then.

'Billie, I'm so, so sorry for what happened with us. I know it's my fault. I know I can never make up to you what happened. I lost you. I'm so sorry for that.'

And suddenly I said, and I never meant to say it, and I never knew I was going to say it. I said . . .

'Let me back, Mum, please,' I said. 'Just let me back, please, I just want to come home.' And I was crying so hard.

'Billie, love,'

'Please, Mum.'

'We tried, Billie, love, you know that. I can cope with them, but I can't cope with you, Billie, and that's all there is to it.'

I pushed the table away. I was crying proper now, I was really crying, and she was crying too, but what does that mean? What's that worth, her tears? Nothing.

'It doesn't mean I don't love you, Billie,' she said. She came towards me with her arms out, but I couldn't bear it any more. I ran to the door, but she got in the way and grabbed me in both hands and pulled me to her.

'It's not fair, let me go, it's not fair you doing this to

me,' I cried. I just wanted to smash her but I couldn't. I couldn't smash my own mum.

'I love you so much,' she whispered in my ear.

I don't think she could have said anything worse to me. Her love – her stupid worthless shitty love!

'How dare you? How fucking dare you!' I screamed, and I shoved her back. She staggered and fell into the cupboards and on to the floor. 'How dare you tell me that, when we both know what shit it is, what useless fucking shit your love is!'

I was gone. There was a mug on the table and I grabbed it and chucked it at her head, but I missed. She scuttled backwards on her hands and feet while I picked up the chair and then, suddenly, Katie was there. Right in front of me. Right in between me and her.

'Go away! Go away!' she was screaming. 'Why can't you just go away? Why can't you just leave us alone? Everything's all right when you're not here. Go away, go away, go away!' she screamed. Her words cut right through me. I wanted to hurt her, but I couldn't, I couldn't. I turned round and ran out, crying on to the street, and crying down the road, because I knew then I'd lost them all forever.

Rob

I had three of the best days of my life, sleeping on a pile of cushions next to my mum's bed. Mum and I hung out during the day while Bridget was at work, and we all sat and watched TV together in the evenings.

Bliss.

As soon as she gets a job, Mum's going to get a place of her own, and I'm coming to live with her – Davey too. It's not so bad for Davey, Philip's OK to him, but I'm pretty sure he'll want to come as well. Then we'll all be together, like it should be.

She's left him before, but I believe her this time. Usually it only lasts a few days. She was away for two weeks once. That's her record. She took me and Davey with her to Aunty Jen's, but then Philip came round and convinced her to come back.

'He's a sweet-talking guy,' she told me. Sweet-talking guy! I couldn't believe she fell for it again. He talks her round every time. She always believes his promises even though he's broken them so many times. *It won't happen again, I love you, I'm so ashamed of myself*, he says – and back she goes. But not this time. This time, she meant it. She'd gone. It didn't matter how much sweet-talking bullshit he fed her. She'd made her mind for good.

She was getting texts from him all the time.

'Here's another one,' she said, about three times a day. And every time my heart would go *flip!*

'What is it this time?' asked Bridget.

'He just wants to talk, he says.'

'Oh, is that all? Well tell him to eff off,' said Bridget and gave me a wink.

Of course it couldn't last.

We were eating a Chinese and watching a Bruce Willis film on TV. I didn't know it, but it was my last evening with her. Philip sent her two more texts during the film. Bridget told her not to bother looking, but she couldn't stop herself.

'Look at this one,' she said. 'He wants me to tell him where I'm staying, so he can forward my post and stuff.'

'Cheeky bugger,' said Bridget. 'He must think you're stupid.'

I was busy stuffing my face with Chinese.

'One thing on my side this time,' said Mum. 'Phil doesn't know where I am. He'd be round here all the time if he knew.'

'Camping on the doorstep,' said Bridget.

'You know what he's like,' said Mum. 'He can talk his way out of anything.'

I just nodded. I wasn't thinking. Then . . . 'Does he know I'm here?' I said.

'Well, of course he does, Rob,' said Mum. 'Where else would you be?'

That was when I realized. It dawned on me, like a punch.

'I can't go back,' I said.

'Robbie . . .'

'I can't. You know what he's like – you said it yourself. He can talk his way out of anything. He'll make me tell him where you are, won't he?'

'Not if you don't tell him,' said Bridget.

'No . . .'

'Robbie, what's the worst that can happen?'

'What'll I do?'

'Are you scared of him, Rob?' asked Bridget.

'No!'

I saw Bridget look at my mum. 'Robbie, tell me,' she said. 'Does Philip hit you? Has he ever?'

'He doesn't hit you, does he, Rob?' said Mum. 'He's always been all right with you, hasn't he?'

Bridget put her hand on Mum's arm to stop her. But . . .

'No, of course he doesn't hit me,' I said.

'He's a bit strict, but he won't hit him – will he, Rob?' said Mum.

'No,' I said. And that was that. The moment was gone.

'But I can't lie to him,' I said. 'You know what he's like. It's not fair.'

'Well, don't lie to him. Just say – just say I told you not to. Tell him. Say it was my wish, and that I said he'd respect it.'

'Yeah, right,' I said. 'And you're scared of him finding out and talking you round, but it's the same for me, isn't it? He can talk me round too, can't he?'

'I know, Rob,' said Mum. 'But you can try. You can try for me, can't you?'

'You can do that for your mum, can't you?' said Bridget.

So it was up to me. Up to me, to protect me mam and look after Davey and stop Philip getting to her. The trouble is, see, what Mum doesn't know is I'm a lump of shite. I let kids half my size bully me. I let bits of shit in the bog jump up and bully me, or I would if they could jump high enough. He wouldn't even need to hit me. He didn't even need to be in the same room. He was turning me into shit right there and then, and he wasn't even in the same *town*.

'Good lad,' said Bridget.

'I know you can do it, love. My big strong boy. Of course you can.'

Does anyone know a magic spell? Because I urgently need one that can turn a lump of shit into a man.

The very next morning she got a text from him saying they wanted me back at the Brant.

'You've got to go, Robbie. You can't stay here forever.'

'Why not? Why can't I?'

'You know why – there's no room.'

'They don't want me back at the Brant. He's lying.'

I really clung on to that one, so she rang up the Brant

and guess what? They did want me back. Can you believe it? The bastards! It was just so they could have a go at me – that's all it was. They didn't want me. Why would they want me back after what I did?

'I might as well stay here till I get let back in school. It's just trouble at the Brant,' I said. 'They just want to have a go at me. I've had enough of a hard time lately,' I begged.

'Oh, love, it's not trouble. They *want* you back.'

'But, Mum . . .'

'It's your education, Robbie. You can't mess around with that. And Bridget's being really good, but we can't impose on her forever, can we?'

'Mum! Please!'

'I'm sorry, love. I've made up my mind. You have to go back.'

It was one of the most miserable days of my life. Mum did her best. On the way we stopped off and she got me a new T-shirt. We couldn't get the fudge-packer one, so she just got me an ordinary Metallica one. It was really nice of her. It just wasn't the same, that's all.

'Now you can get rid of that horrible old one,' she told me.

'No way!' I said. I'd told her how important that T-shirt was, but she obviously hadn't been listening to a word I'd told her. That T-shirt, it was my *soul*.

'Robbie.' She stepped in front of me, which she always does when she wants to make an impression. 'Do you want me down here worrying every minute of every day because of you and a stupid old T-shirt?'

'It's not just a T-shirt . . .'

'I know how important it is to you, but you can't spend the rest of your life getting beat up because of it. Put it in a drawer or something. Save it for concerts or something. Wear this one at school. You have enough problems as it is. All right? Promise me, promise me now.'

So I did. Only my mum, only for her. It shows she's thinking of me, doesn't it?

I don't know how I did the bus ride home. I never felt so depressed. School, home, the Brant, there was no let-up to it. I'd been putting up with it for long enough. I don't know why it was so hard. You'd think it'd get easier. I suppose because I'd had a taste of being with Mum, away from it all. All the way home I had my phone in my hand and I kept thinking how easy it would be to press Mum's number and ring her up and say . . . 'Mum, I can't do it, Mum. I just can't do it, because, the way he beats me up, it's just not right.' That's all I had to do. If I did that there's no way on this earth she'd let me go back to him.

But I couldn't do it. If I said that, it'd be like saying, 'Your boyfriend has been beating up your son all these years and you never even knew it.' That's like saying what a bad mother you are. You can't do that to your own mum, now can you?

Back home, I wanted to get up to my bedroom without being seen, but Philip called me from the front room. He was sat there with Davey playing on my

Xbox. They'd taken it down and wired it up to the big TV. We were never allowed to do that when I'd been there.

Davey said hi, but he didn't look happy. Playing on the Xbox with your dad, that must be a nice thing. Even Philip must have felt a bit bad because he lifted up his handset and shook it at me.

'Want a go?' he said.

'No thanks. I'm tired. I'm going to bed,' I said. No one complained when I left.

Davey came up a bit afterwards and tried to explain about the Xbox.

'We just thought,' he said, 'you not being here . . .'

'Keep it. I won't be needing it again,' I told him.

'Don't be like that, Rob. I won't play it with him any more if you like.'

'I don't care, Davey.'

'Rob . . .'

'Just leave me alone, will you? I need you to leave me alone, Davey. OK?'

He stood there awhile. Then he cleared off downstairs. Philip must have been pissed off with him for something, because there were raised voices. It turned out that Davey wasn't playing with him any more and, of course, Philip could guess why. See? Rob goes away and Davey gets on with his dad. Rob comes back and they fall out. A bad-luck charm. That's all I am. Everything I do goes wrong.

I lay there for a long time. Then I got up and took off the fudge-packer T-shirt. I folded it up carefully and put it in a carrier bag under my bed. I'd promised me mam. It was like the power was leaving me. Then I went back to lie on my bed again, and tried to go to sleep.

Hannah

The thing about this job is you never know what you're going to get. I'm always being surprised. Sometimes, I'm actually amazed. Our kids have all got issues, but at least they're characters. There's more character in one of our classrooms than in most whole schools.

On the other hand, you can't like them all.

I know it sounds unfair, but that's the way it is. It's the bullies I can't cope with. I hadn't realized with Rob when he came in at first. There was that weird thing about the T-shirt – what was that about? Heavy metal. I don't like the music. You try and give people the benefit of the doubt, but maybe it follows that I don't like the people either.

He came back in that Monday morning, and everyone in the building wanted his blood. Jim had a go at him first. You could hear it all down the corridor.

'I like to believe that there's a purpose for everyone in this world, Rob, but I'm finding it very difficult to work out just what yours is. Unless it's causing trouble for other people. Am I getting through here?'

He can lay it on a bit thick, can Jim. Then Melanie had a go at him, then a couple of the other teachers. God knows what the kids were like – Billie was a hero to them. Well, enough was enough. I was going to leave him alone, but I was that angry about what he'd done to Billie. She'd only gone and run off again. This was a bad one. Usually she settles after throwing a wobbly. The trouble is she'd lost everything now. This was the big one – and it was all because of this idiot.

I hoiked him into my office during break. I couldn't help myself.

'It was an accident,' he said.

'You pulled down her trousers by accident?'

'Yeah.'

'Don't treat me like an idiot, Rob.'

'I'm not, miss.'

'How is it possible to pull down a girl's trousers by accident?'

'You trip over something, miss. Miss. I'd never do anything like that to Billie. I like her.'

'Is that how you show a girl you like her? By pulling down her trousers in public?'

He pulled a face.

'I would imagine that the next time you see Billie it won't be a very friendly encounter. Did you know that she was on her last chance here? And I don't mean her last chance. I mean her last last chance?'

'I know. She told me.'

'Well, she's blown that now, hasn't she? With your help. We can't let her back in here. Chris's parents are pressing assault charges on her. Maybe even Actual Bodily Harm.'

To my satisfaction, he looked horrified. I nodded. 'Did you know she's gone on the run? Did you know that?' He shook his head. 'I don't blame her for running, either,' I went on. 'She'll be off to the LOK now. Secure after that, more likely than not. With a record. Well done, Rob. You're a pretty good friend to have around, aren't you? I just hope for your sake that Billie doesn't show her gratitude too forcefully.'

He didn't say anything, just sloped off. Friends with Billie! I ask you. You believe that, you'll believe anything. Manipulative as well as a bully. Well – there must be something to like about that kid, but for the life of me I can't see it.

On the other hand, there was Chris Trent. After what happened, the school decided to take him back in. But then I made my way down at break on Friday morning – and there he was drinking tea and eating toast with the others. I did a complete double-take. The other kids were all clustered round him like he was some kind of big cheese – having your balls crushed by Billie evidently conferred some sort of glamour.

'Chris,' I said. 'What are you doing here?'

I didn't get any further than that. Jim popped his head out of the door and beckoned me over.

'You're not going to believe this,' he said.

So it turns out that Chris and Billie made friends when she went round to the hospital. Somehow, he'd managed to talk his parents into dropping the charges. I could hardly believe my ears. Neither could Jim. He'd had to ring the police and check it out before he believed it.

'They were furious about it,' he said. 'They thought they had her this time.'

Billie! You jammy cow. How many lives has that girl got? But it wasn't jammy, was it? She went to say she was sorry. See, Billie? You're getting it right. You've given yourself another chance. All you have to do is take it. I had my phone out to call her, but she wasn't picking up, so I texted her instead – 'Billie, they've dropped the charges. Ring me now!'

'But he still shouldn't be here, should he?' I told Jim.

Jim scratched his face. 'He's supposed to be at school,' he admitted. 'But . . . he wants to be here.'

I shrugged. 'Since when did we let kids come here on demand?' I asked.

'Since they do things like that?' said Jim.

'But the school'll be wanting to know where he is,' I said. Technically, we were complicit in helping him truant. 'What about his parents? Do they know?'

Jim shrugged. 'I haven't found the time to ring them yet,' he said. 'Busy morning. I'm assuming there's some sort of cock-up going on.'

'. . . And you're not trying too hard to sort it out.'

'. . . Not too hard.'

Jim, we have our disagreements, but his heart's in the right place. I thought, *Chris, you little darling!* I could have run out and kissed him there and then.

*

See what I mean? The Chrises and the Robs. The good, the bad and the ugly. We try to offer them a good service in terms of keeping up with their work, but they're often so far behind it's a waste of time. Rob was one of those. When Melanie got in touch with his form teacher to ask about work, he just laughed at her. There wasn't much point in making him do lessons – he was only here for a couple of weeks – so he came to me to do some PD. Personal development.

A lot of the kids think PD is just a doddle. So it is – up to a point. It's just games. You might do a drawing of yourself or write down what your good points are and what your bad points are and then afterwards everyone gets to talk about their choices. The kids all sit around looking bored more often than not. But, the thing is, talking about your good points and your bad points is a way of talking about yourself. It's a way in. Before you know it, someone starts talking about what's going on at home or at school or whatever. And with a bit of luck – out it all comes.

You'd be amazed at the things some of our kids have to put up with. People see them as troublemakers, but if you knew the trouble that's going on in their lives you wouldn't think like that. Imagine it. Your mum's on the bottle and the baby needs looking after. Or your dad's in prison and your mum's depressed, there's no money. Under those circumstances, if you're a responsible person, school isn't going to be your first priority, is it? Your brothers and sisters need feeding, the baby's hungry – and you're spending your day sitting in a classroom putting your education first? Would you put school at the top of your list if that was your life? I certainly wouldn't. And then when you do go in, you're treated like some kind of delinquent brat.

Those kids, to me, they're not troublemakers – they're heroes. Proper, real-life heroes. Giving up their chances in life to make sure that the people who are important to them are properly cared for – that's heroic, isn't it? And what do they get for it? The whole system comes down on them like a ton of bricks.

And then of course you also get the ones who are just useless lumps of trouble. You try to learn which ones are which. And, with a bit of experience, you can tell. Or you think you can.

And then you get taken down a peg or two.

We were doing a game called Futures. You write down what your dream for the future is. That's it. Simple. Rob wanted to be a drummer in a death-metal band. Chris was in there, too. He wanted to be an entrepreneur and he was being a pain. He kept helping people.

'Chris, what are you doing?'

'I'm helping Maheed.'

'Maheed, do you need any help?'

'No, miss.'

'Chris, let me repeat the question. What are you doing?'

'I'm being helpful,' he said.

'No, you're not. Helpful is when you do something people need. There's no one in this room needs any help writing down a simple sentence saying what their dreams are. OK?'

'All right, all right, keep your hair on.'

Irritating, when he puts his mind to it. Helpful and irritating? What's that about?

I got back to Rob.

'You play drums, then, do you, Rob?' I asked him.

'Used to,' he said.

'Oh, what happened?'

He shrugged. 'Me dad got rid of them.'

'Why'd he do that?' I said.

Robbie smiled. 'He said I was making a racket,' he confessed. Everyone laughed. I waited. 'Anyway,' he said defensively. 'He isn't me real dad; he's just a stepdad.' And then he looked sideways at me and –

I know that look. I thought, *Right*.

We finished the session and I asked him to stay over. He didn't like it, but he did as I asked. I waited till the rest of them had gone and I said, 'I was just thinking, Rob, I don't know anything about you really, do I?'

'Nothing to know,' he said.

'So, tell me, how's things at home?'

'All right.'

'What's the set-up?'

He began to talk, slowly at first. About his mum moving out, leaving him behind with his brother and his stepdad. Then a load of stuff about how great his mum was. My God, she was some kind of superwoman, this mum of his. Nothing about his stepdad, though, or any blame for her for going off and leaving him. Just how great she was for buying him a T-shirt.

Buying him a T-shirt means that much?

'And how does your brother get on with your stepdad?'

'Pretty good. He's his proper dad.'

'Is he happy about your mum going?'

I asked a few more questions. Rob picked up a pencil and started doodling away, like he was bored. But, I knew, he wasn't bored.

And then I struck pay dirt. 'And how do you get on with your stepdad, then?'

Slowly at first. His dad going when he was small. Philip moving in. Philip scaring his mum. Scaring him.

Scaring him. I took a leap in the dark. 'Rob. Is he hurting you?'

'No,' he said. 'No, he wouldn't do that.'

And then he started to cry.

Oh, Christ. Rob not telling his mum because he wants to look after her. Thinking that so long as Philip's on his back he won't hurt his mum or his brother. Carrying the whole mess on his own shoulders. I didn't push it. I just let him talk. And talk and talk and talk. Nothing about being hurt – he wasn't going to admit that, if that's what it was. But all about how great his mum was and how bad Philip was, and how much he wanted to help her and how much he hated him. It took about fifteen minutes, I'd say. Light the blue touchpaper and stand back.

After he'd done, I leaned back and I said, 'OK, Rob,

I want to tell you how hearing that makes me feel, if that's all right.' He looked at me like I'd slapped him.

'What?' he said.

'It makes me feel very, very angry that you're being treated like that. It makes me feel very sad that there's no one there to help you out and take that load off your shoulders. And another thing it makes me feel: it makes me feel a whole lot of respect for you, Rob.'

He looked at me like – respect? It had never occurred to him that anything he did was worth respecting.

'The way you look after your little brother. I don't know if I could do that. You must get very angry with him sometimes, because he's the favourite. But instead of taking it out on Davey, you look out for him. No wonder he loves you so much. No wonder your mum trusts you so much to keep an eye out for him.'

'Yeah, well,' he muttered. He looked astonished. But I meant every word.

'And not telling your mum how much Philip bullies you – that's really brave,' I said. He hadn't said a word about being bullied, but he didn't disagree.

'I do have a problem with it, mind. Protecting your mum, that's not your job. It's not fair on you. But I have so much respect for you, Rob, for your courage, for your faith in people. You're a hero. No, I mean it. You have all these troubles on your shoulders, at home, at school, here – and there you are, looking after the people who mean something to you. Not lashing out at them, not causing them trouble – taking care of the people you love. I can't tell you how much respect I have for that.'

'Yeah, well,' he muttered. He looked so embarrassed, poor love. But then I got my reward. He peeped up and smiled at me – a great big smile.

Put me in my place, eh?

We talked a little longer. I've not got it all out of him, not by a mile – but it's a start. I got his records out. Moved here from Manchester just a few months ago. Wonder what the story is behind that? Excluded for bullying. I know that school. They have a culture of bullying there. I should have had my alarm bells ringing about this right at the start. Sometimes, it's easier for the school to get rid of the kid who's being bullied, rather than take on the whole culture. That way they only have to deal with one kid and not half the students there. Not to mention the teachers. I'll bet my bottom dollar that's what's happened with our Rob.

He should be coming here full time. I'll have a word with Jim to get on to the school, and see what we can do for him.

There we go. Another lesson, another kid. Hero or troublemaker? You tell me. Maybe it's the same thing.

After Rob had left I went round and gathered everyone's papers together and had a quick look. They'd all written something, except – guess who? Chris Trent. Now, that was a surprise. There was his name, nice and neat at the top. Rest of the paper – blank. I thought, *You lazy little get. Anything to get out of doing any work, is that it, Chris?* I might have left it there, but . . . what about all that fuss in class earlier? Fidgeting in his chair. Helping everyone whether they need it or not. He'd been more trouble than the rest of them put together.

I went and checked his notes. I was amazed. His work in school was pretty patchy, but it was the homework. He hadn't done any for *four years*. Nothing. They'd tried every measure on earth to get him to do the work, and he refused to shift. That's pretty committed laziness, isn't it? So what's that about? Principles? You reckon?

Because I don't.

I'd call that more like a cry for help.

Rob

I was having a day and a half. First everyone's having a go at me about Billie and suddenly there's Hannah telling me how great I am. I don't get it. It was nice, but – she doesn't know what a coward I am. I wasn't going to tell her, either.

Philip was on my case as soon as I got up that first morning after I got back. 'Where is she, son?' he said. I hate it when he calls me son. I said what Mum told me to say – that she'd asked me not to tell him and that she said he'd respect her wishes. He nodded, but that didn't mean anything. We were at breakfast; Davey was there. But the look he gave me. It's not over, no way is it over. Tonight, tomorrow night, sometime very soon, he's going to ask me again and I'm going to tell him. I'm not a hero. My mum is the hero. She's the one who's trying to save us all from Philip. I'm the one who's going to blow it for her.

See how much Hannah respects me when that happens.

Even so, she made me feel better. And then I wasn't

out of there ten minutes when – guess what? Snail-boy. Would you believe it? He comes straight up to me while I'm eating my crisps in a nice quiet corner and he goes, 'Right. I don't like you and you don't like me.'

'Look, mate,' I said. 'I don't want any trouble. I've had it with trouble. I'm sorry you got your balls stamped on. Can we just leave it now, OK?'

'It's not that,' he said. 'That fight with Billie. You know what happened, don't you?'

'What?'

'You were tripped up.'

'You're joking!'

'I'm not.'

'On purpose?'

'Yeah.'

It made sense – the way I went down.

'Who was it?'

'That kid Ed.'

I breathed out. 'Him.'

'Yeah.'

'The most irritating kid in the world.'

'Yeah.'

We stood there looking at each other. I'd had my head kicked in, he'd had his balls stamped on, all because of that one nerdy little kid.

'What do you want to do?' he said.

'I want to kick his head in. You?'

'You're on.'

We caught up with him later in the toilets – it's about

the only place you can get someone in the Brant. He tried to make a run between us, but we cut him off.

'I'll tell Jim,' he squeaked. 'I'll tell Hannah!'

'Tell who you want,' said Chris, and he shoved him back inside. We cornered him by the wash basin. He was just this miserable little squirt. It was pathetic.

'What are we going to do with him?' asked Chris.

'Pulverize him,' I said.

'I had your mum,' said Ed.

Chris and I looked at each other.

'What?' we both said.

'I had your mum,' he squeaked. Then he looked up at us and smirked.

What? Did he want to get beaten up? Why was he making it worse? He was supposed to be begging for mercy and whimpering and crying.

'Are you off your head?' said Chris.

'I had your sister and all,' he said.

We looked at each other over the top of his head.

'He is, he's mental,' I said.

We picked him up by the shirt, but, funny thing, no one did anything yet. It was just too pathetic. Him almost begging for it. It made hitting the little weed just . . . I dunno . . .

'Bog wash?' suggested Chris.

'What's that?'

'Head down the toilet, flush the chain.'

'Good. No! He'll be wet, they'll know.'

'Your mum liked it! She asked me to do it again!' he screeched.

I reached down and wriggled my fingers in Ed's side, and the kid whooped.

'No! Don't do that!' he yelled.

So we grabbed him tight, got him face up on the floor, held his arms above his head, sat on his legs and tickled the little runt and he laughed and laughed and laughed so much he was sick. At least, he would have been if Jim hadn't come in. We got a good few minutes in, though, I reckon. He was pretty nearly weeping by then.

Jim was furious.

'I won't have fighting in here,' he yelled.

The little toad scrambled to his feet. 'They beat me up, sir. They bog-washed me. They said they'd had my mum, sir.'

'Get out, Ed, I don't believe a word of it,' said Jim. Ed ran off.

He turned on me. 'You. I might have known it,' he said.

'But Ed tripped him up, Jim,' said Chris. 'That's why he pulled down Billie's trousers. It wasn't Rob's fault – it was that kid Ed tripping him up.'

Jim looked at me. Then he closed his eyes for a moment. 'Is this true?'

'Ask anyone, sir. They all saw it.'

'I might have known,' he said. 'Why didn't you tell me this earlier?'

'He's dangerous, that kid,' said Chris. There was a pause. 'Sorry, Jim,' he added.

'Right. You did someone in here a favour recently, Chris, so I'm letting you off. Just this once. The rules is the rules. I make 'em, you keep 'em. Now we're quits. OK?'

'Understood.'

'Good. Now get out of my sight.'

Chris ducked out and he turned his attention to me.

'You broke an important rule, Robbie. I understand why you broke that rule, so this incident is not going any further than this toilet. I'm giving you one more chance. Understand?'

'Right!'

'Don't let me down! No matter what happens at home, this *is* a safe place. Not that I'm having much luck in that direction lately, but still. Understood?'

'Understood.'

'Now get out of my sight, and don't let me find you in any more trouble again – ever!'

And I went, quick, before he changed his mind.

I'm not often in a good mood these days but the Brant was OK that day. I like Hannah, she's all right. She said she was going to try and take me out of school, which would have seemed like a bad thing only a few days ago, but now it sounded like common sense. Jim the head had let me off. There were people actually on my side.

And I was mates with Snailboy! We spent the rest of the day hanging out together, killing ourselves laughing. It was great. I have a new mate! How about that? Who would have thought it? Snailboy, king of molluscs, and me. Amazing!

*

Back at home I played Davey on the Xbox in my room, let him win. We had egg and chips for tea, one of my favourites. We watched a bit of telly. Philip was OK. He was seeing that woman again. Maybe he'd moved on too. Maybe he wasn't going to bother trying to find out where Mum lived. You never know. I went to bed thinking maybe my luck had finally changed. I woke up and there he was, sitting by the edge of the bed.

'What?' I said. I was dozy. I didn't know what was going on. It felt like the middle of the night and he smelled of beer, but he didn't seem angry or anything. Just sitting there in a chair he'd pulled up next to the bed, watching me.

'You awake?' he asked.

'I am now,' I muttered.

He nodded. He had his tobacco tin out and he was rolling one up on his knee.

'It's time we had a little chat,' he said. He smiled at me. 'Me and you,' he said. He sat up and put his lighter to his ciggie and peered at me through the smoke. 'We've had our differences, Rob, but I'm still your step-dad. I'm your dad, really, like your mum says. I've been around that long. We have our fights, but that's normal between father and son.' He nodded and looked at me and waited for me to nod back. And that's what I did. And, as I did, a little bit of me turned to shit.

'I want to tell you, Robbie,' he said, 'how much I appreciate how you keep an eye out for Davey. It's really good knowing that I can rely on you. A lot of big brothers'd take against the smaller one, especially when it's a step-family. I know things can be hard. I know that. There are resentments and things. But you handle it really well. I admire you for that. Sometimes I let things get the better of me, especially when I've had a few, but you're a good lad. Yeah,' he went on, nodding in the smoky light. 'We do all right. We've had our differences, but underneath it's all right. You know?'

He waited for me to nod again. So I did. And another little piece of me turned into shit.

Magician of shit.

'You're a good lad,' he said again. He took another drag. 'Your mum going off like that – it must have been a shock for you, eh?'

'I didn't know she was going.'

'Neither did I. Well, I did on the night. Rob, I have to say, I'm sorry for the way I came back with Silvia that time. It was wrong of me. I was that angry I didn't know what I was doing.'

He took another drag of his fag. All the time, he never took his eyes off me.

'But what she did was wrong as well,' he said. 'Just taking off like that. Not telling you. I thought you knew, that morning, did you know that? I knew she'd been in to see you.'

'She had been in but she didn't say. I don't know why she didn't.'

'It was wrong of her. The thing is, Robbie, she doesn't appreciate you enough. I know she wants to get a place of her own, and when she does she wants you and Davey to go and live with her. But I'm going to fight that, Robbie. She's not taking my son away from me. I'll win too. She's the one who's deserted the family home – deserted her two sons and her husband. The court isn't going to look right well on that. Davey will stay here, and I'm going to need you here as well to help me with him. Keep an eye on him. Poor little lad, with no mother – he needs you, Robbie. I want you to promise me. Will you do that for me, Robbie – for Davey? I want you to promise you're going to stay here with us.'

He looked at me and smiled.

'I want your word,' he said softly. 'I mean it, Rob. I want your word.'

'I promise.' And as I spoke those words my heart turned into shit.

'Say it. Say you promise you'll stay here with me and Davey. Go on, say it.'

'I promise,' I said. 'I promise I'll stay here with you and Davey.'

'And not go and live with your mum.'

'And not go to live with my mum,' I said.

Then he leaned in close, the creepy bastard, and he said, 'Because she doesn't love you enough.'

I looked at him and he looked at me. He knew exactly what he was asking me to do.

'Say it,' he said. 'It's the truth – we both know it. We might as well get it out. Say it. "Because she doesn't love me enough."'

'I can't . . .'

'You can. You will. Now. Say it.'

'Because my mum doesn't love me enough,' I said. And my whole body and soul . . .

And I began to cry.

I'm sorry, Mum. I'm so sorry. I can't stop him making me do things.

'Good boy,' he said. 'And now I want you downstairs.'

I got out of bed in my boxers, pulled a T-shirt on. I was going to get dressed, but he told me not to bother. I followed him down.

I don't know why I do what he wants. Sometimes I think maybe it's because of what he'll do if I don't, but that's stupid, because in the end we both know he's going to do it anyway.

He had his mate Alan there. They'd been drinking. There were full ashtrays and the table was covered in beer cans. On the settee there was a street map of Manchester spread out.

'Now,' he said. 'I want to know where she is. I want to know where the mother of my child is hiding from me. I want to know now. And you're going to tell me.'

PART 3

The Band

Billie

I meant to go back to Barbara after, but I couldn't face it. I couldn't face Hannah, either, or Sue and Jane or anyone, so I spent the night in a derri on Charles Street hiding out in one of the bedrooms upstairs. I'd been there before with some friends. It was crap; we only did it just to see. But on my own it was really miserable. In the night, some guys turned up, dead drunk. Homeless. Four or five dirty old drunks and me on my own? They could do anything. I just kept as quiet as I could and hoped no one would come upstairs. They fell asleep in the end, but I didn't dare leave in the dark, I was that scared.

That was my lowest night ever, lying up in that room listening to those down-and-outs, after Mum said no to me again. There was a woman with them, out of her head, cursing and shouting. I think some of the guys had a go at her in the night. It was, like, that was me. I was listening in on what I had to come. I thought about Hannah. I thought about Barbara too, and how I could have been tucked up safe in that silly little room. If I'd had my phone with me, I might have rung one of them, but what for? I'd run out of options.

I got out in the morning once the cars started up outside. I didn't see any of the drunks. I just pushed open the front door and ran out. I wasn't planning on spending another night like that. No way, but I wasn't ready to go back to Barbara's, either. They want to lock me up, let them catch me.

I went round to see Cookie instead.

It was early. He was still in bed, I had to go round and rap on the window. And rap. And rap and rap and rap.

'Come on, you bastard, wake up,' I was hissing. Then his face loomed up in the window and he staggered off to open the door.

Cookie, he's an ugly bugger at the best of times. He stood there at the door in his boxers like something that had just crawled out of the dog's nose.

'What?'

'Can I come in?'

He hobbled to one side. I went to the kitchen. He shut the door and followed me through.

'What?' he said again.

'Can you put me up for a few days?'

'What?'

'Just a few days. I got a spot of bother. I put this lad in hospital.'

'Jesus.'

'Just for a few days.'

Cookie shook his head. '. . . Back to bed,' he muttered. He staggered off, leaving me standing there.

'Thanks – thanks!' I called after him. He waved a hand and disappeared towards the bedroom.

Somewhere to stay.

I went straight to the fridge. Nothing there, but I found burgers in the freezer and a load of buns he'd nicked from work. Burgers and Cookie. He works with them, he eats them, he smells like them, he even tastes like them. I got a couple out and stuck them in the microwave. I looked around while I waited. It was a shithole. Grease everywhere, sink clogged up with paper plates – he nicks them from work too – and fag ends and beer cans. It smelled of rotting meat. He'd had a heavy night.

Cookie called out from the bedroom.

'Billie!'

'What?'

'Come here.'

'What?'

'No, come here.'

I went through. He was lying under the duvet, no cover on it, just this cheap duvet.

He didn't look good. He didn't smell good, either.

He lifted up the duvet.

'I got . . .'

'Gerrin!'

'But . . .'

'Gerrin!'

Yeah, well. You got to pay your rent. I got in, but it

wasn't that. He lay on his stomach and turned his face away, maybe so I wouldn't have to smell his breath, and he put an arm round my neck and hoiked me up to him. That was all. I put my arm over his shoulders and my leg over his bum and closed my eyes. I was starving. I heard the burgers ping in the microwave, but I didn't move. I just lay there, feeling his warmth, until I fell asleep.

Hannah

She hasn't even got her phone on her – can you believe that? She always has her phone on her. Barbara's left it out on the kitchen table and I was sure she'd drop back to pick it up, but no. I said I'd be there for her – but how can you be there for someone if you don't know where they are? I am so going to kill that girl when I get my hands on her. If someone else hasn't done it for me first, that is.

You think I'm joking? We haven't had any murders among the young people who come here – so far. We've had everything else, though. Rape, GBH, abduction, prostitution, drug addiction, suicide attempts – suicide successes. Which one do you think Billie is most likely to fall for?

None of them would surprise me. They all happen, and they all happen to girls like Billie.

But . . . What can you do? Only your best. And life goes on, with or without Billie Trevors. I have other people to worry about apart from her. I'm not the only one obsessing about her, either. I had Rob in here the other day in a state about her. I'd asked everyone at the Brant to keep an eye out for her, and he was in my office straight off. I thought he was just scared she was going to kill him for pulling down her trousers – with good reason. And he is. But . . . it's a little more than that.

Once he'd found out she doesn't even know the charges have been dropped, that was it, he was on a mission. She had to be found and he was going to find her. It was Rob on the job. Before school, after school. Lunch break, weekends . . .

'Rob,' I said. 'Any help I can get looking for Billie is great – but get on with your own life as well, OK? It's good that you've made friends with Chris. Hang out with him a bit. You can't spend your whole time looking for Billie.'

'But she needs our help,' he said.

Not content with rescuing his mum, he wants to rescue Billie as well. A knight in shining armour, that's our Rob. All wide eyes and optimism and full of hope. God only knows what he's been through, and there he is, still expecting the world to come out right. How do you tell them that it's not always like that without turning them into cynics? Plan for the worst, hope for the best, that's what I try to get across. But it's a hard lesson to get right.

'I'm not saying don't look for her, Rob. I'm just saying you don't know how it'll work out. Don't put too much hope into rescuing someone. You can't always do it and, sometimes, they don't even want it.'

He looked at me and scowled. 'But you've been out looking for her too, haven't you?' he said. And I thought, *Yeah, you know what, Hannah? When are you going to learn to take your own advice?*

Get a life.

No chance. How do you think I've time for anything like that when I have this lot to think about?

'Just do your own thing as well, Rob. Look, have you been down to the Corn Exchange yet on a Saturday afternoon? That's where all the kids hang out. I think you should go. Take Chris. Ask Ruth about it. She goes. You might find some kindred spirits there.'

'But you will tell me if there's any news about Billie, won't you?'

'I will. Now scram. I have work to do.'

I'm happy with progress with Rob. He's doing really well – looks a lot happier than when he first came, anyway. I'm not at the bottom of it yet, not by a long way. But we're getting there. Which is more than I can say about his mate. What is going on with Chris Trent? I can't get any kind of handle on him at all. And clever? He's like a psychological version of Muhammad bloody Ali. You can't get near him. We had a call from his school on Wednesday morning, when they cottoned on he was still with us. So that was going to be our last day with him. I decided to try something out. I got him after lunch as he was coming back into lessons.

'A word, Chris.'

'I've got Mrs Robbins for cookery.'

'You can make your biscuits later.'

We went up to my office. I took out a small wodge of paper and spread the pages out on the desk in front of me.

'This is your work, Chris. Your entire output in three days here at the Brant.'

We sat and looked at them. There were about seven sheets of paper. Five of them just had his name written neatly in the top right-hand corner. One of them had the word 'Twelve' written on the top line. The last sheet had the word 'Arse' written in capitals filled in with blue biro about halfway down.

Chris smiled fondly at it. 'That's my favourite,' he said.

'Yeah, I expect you need the context to get the joke,' I said. 'What I want to know is – you explained to me why you don't do homework. How come you're not doing anything in class either?'

'No point, is there?' he said. 'I'm not planning on getting any qualifications. You don't need them in my line.'

'I see. So, tell me. If you had your choice, what would you be doing in school?'

'If I had a choice? Dream on! But I guess, really, I'd like to be doing some work on my eBay shop.'

I got him set up. Stan, who does our tech, opened up eBay for him – it's off-limits normally, same as Facebook and so on – and I put him to work.

Impressive, I have to say. Posting images from his phone, checking prices with other traders, doing a few sums. Cutting and pasting. I've no doubt he's going to make a lot of money one day.

'How about writing up some ads about the products, then, Chris?' I said.

'No point. No assets. They froze my account.'

'Do it anyway. Just for me.'

'No! I don't like people looking over my shoulder.'

'You didn't mind with the pictures and so on.'

'That's different.'

Yeah, isn't it? I looked at him and he looked at me. I gave him my sweetest smile.

'OK, Chris, thanks for that. Now then, I've got a little test I want you to do, and then you can go.'

'What for?'

'Oh, just for our records. It won't take long. Half an hour.'

He didn't like it. He didn't like it even more when I sat down opposite him and got on with my work while he did it. He was writhing around like a cauldron full of snakes. It took him ages. I thought he was going to walk out at one point, but he got through it in the end. Most of it anyway.

'Right, thanks. You can go now.'

He got up and slouched off. 'See you later,' I called.

'Yeah.' He was watching me suspiciously. Well he might. I had a quick look through his papers after and then went back to his online shop. The shop was beautifully done. Attractive to look at, easy to use. I'll buy something myself off it when it's up and running again. Word perfect too. No spelling mistakes, no repetitions. Grammar. Everything right. Unlike the papers he'd just filled in for me.

Gotcha.

Chris

I managed to last a whole week at home after coming out of hospital. It still amazes me that it worked at all, actually. The way my mum and dad just fell into my pocket. Maybe it was because they were making a deal. They so badly wanted to get the cuffs on Billie they must have felt I *owed* it to them to tell the truth for dropping the charges. Yes, Mum and Dad – I'll go to school. Yes, I'll get on with the homework. Yes, I'll never run away and live in a tent again, not even the two-man tent you don't know about, hidden in the garage. Promise.

You'd have thought even a half-wit would have realized that at least a part of that was bound to be not true, if not all. But no. They swallowed the lot.

I had another day off at home, which was crazy because I was fine really. I spent the time usefully though, smuggling out the two-man tent to a top-secret location. I was going up the wall by the evening, so they let me get back to school on Friday. Of course I didn't stay there. It took some planning, mind.

I went to school for registration, creating the illusion of attendance. Then I left before lessons and went down the Brant to give Jim and Hannah the glad news about Billie, where I was greeted like a hero. Much better than school, thanks. I followed up on Monday morning by ringing the school, as my dad, saying how poor Chris had gone back to hospital for more tests. The receptionist was very sweet about it – wished poor Chris luck and said how much they were all missing him and hoped to see him soon.

Yeah, right.

It lasted till Wednesday. Jim had tipped me off that the school had cottoned on, and I knew Mum and Dad had been told as soon as I got home after my last day. They were waiting for me, both of 'em at the kitchen table. I peered in through the window. You could tell from their faces. They were disappointed. They were angry. They were . . . out of their depth.

Dad caught sight of me peering in, and if I hadn't have known I soon would have done by the way he reacted.

'There he is now!' he yelled. They both jumped up and ran out of the back door, Dad shouting and yelling at me, Mum shouting and yelling at Dad. Me? I was on my bike. Literally. They'd both been so pleased when I started cycling to school. They should have known better. I simply turned the bike round and swooshed off. They rushed into the street behind me as I sailed away like an eagle towards the main road.

'*That's* why he was riding the bike – he's been planning this all along!' my dad yelled.

'Don't be ridiculous,' hissed my mother – who, despite all the evidence, refused to believe just how cunning I was prepared to be.

Once I was sure I was safe, I stopped and turned round to look. They were standing in the road, the losers, watching their only hope of passing on their ridiculous genes to another generation disappear beyond their eyes.

'Ah am prepared to follow you to the ends of time,' I called back, in a heavy cod-American accent. 'In ma efforts to ensure that you and your progeny do not continue to pollute God's good earth.'

They just stood there and stared. Then I lifted my foot off the ground and wheeled off into the sunset.

Rob

Get on this.

I lied.

It's so easy to say those two little words. I. Lied. Simple. We do it all the time. We don't even think about it. But not for me, not to him. Not about something like that.

I didn't have the courage to face him down and just say no. I don't think I'll ever be that brave. But I lied. Him and his mate stood there looking at me while I stared at that map. I could see the street, I could almost see the house in my mind. I put my finger out – and I plumped it down on another street miles away.

'Number five,' I said.

It was the bravest thing I've ever done. Bar none. And ever since that day I have been living in fear. Every time I come back from the Brant, I'm thinking, *Has he been there?* Every time he goes out and starts up the car, I'm thinking, *Is he going there now?*

He will find out. I know that. He'll go looking for her, all the way to Manchester, and he'll find the street that I pointed to and he'll knock on the door and someone he's never seen is going to open that door to him. And then he'll get back in the car, drive all the way home and he'll kick my brains in. And then – then I'm going to tell him the truth.

I know that too. Those facts – he's going to find out that I lied and he's going to kick my brains in and he's going to make me tell the truth. That's my world. All I've done is put it off. I am going to betray the woman who gave birth to me. It's just a matter of when.

So – what's new? Philip's going to kick my head in. So what? He always was. It's going to happen whether I lie or whether I say nothing or whether I tell him the truth. There's no point in worrying about stuff that's going to happen anyway. But today – today it's Saturday. Right now, I'm on my way to meet Chris. Not getting my head kicked in by Philip, or Martin Riley, or anyone else. We're going to look for Billie and then we're off into Leeds to meet the freaks. When I get home tonight, Philip will probably have gone to Manchester, and he'll have found out, and he'll kick my head in. Then, I'll be a piece of shit. But right now, right this minute, just for a few hours, I'm not a piece of shit. For once, I'm just me.

Right?

Right.

I've been thinking about things lately and do you know what I've realized? I am actually one lucky guy. I've been going on about how crap my life is, but there's plenty of people have it worse than me. What about Billie? Did you know her mother doesn't even want to live with her? When Hannah told me that, I could not believe my ears.

'Her mum?' I kept saying. How can your mum not want you? I cannot even begin to imagine what it must be like to have a mother who doesn't love you – who doesn't even want you in the same house! Now that is bad.

There she is, on the run, all on her own, no one to love her, still thinking Chris is pressing charges . . . and no mother to turn to when she needs her.

No matter what else happens to me in this world, I know my mother loves me. Whether she gets it right or wrong, she will always love me and I will always love and honour her for everything she's done for me.

I told Hannah right then I'm going to do everything I can to find her. I've been out every evening. That's no hardship; it keeps me away from Philip. And lunch times and mornings. I've been asking around. It turns out Chris lives just round the corner to where she used to hang out. I've seen her in that park a few times. So me and Chris, we've been round there a few times together, seeing if she still is.

And just in case you're wondering – no, I don't fancy her. Even if I did, she wouldn't go out with me, would she? She's got enough on her plate. I just like her, that's all.

And if I did – I wouldn't tell you anyway, would I?

*

I asked Ruth about the Corn Exchange in Leeds, like Hannah said.

'You want to meet the freaks, eh?' said Ruth.

'I don't know if I want to be a freak,' I told her.

She lifted up my top and pointed to the T-shirt. 'Too late, you are one,' she told me.

It was the second T-shirt, not the really sacred one. But she's right. I am a freak. My music is freak music, my tastes are freak tastes. Like Ruth says, if you're gonna be a freak you might as well do it in company. And you never know – maybe we'd see Billie there as well. Because, let's face it – she's a freak too.

I met up with Chris in the park. He didn't want to meet at his house. Can you believe he's actually camping out rather than live at home? His dad must be a real monster. He has this two-man tent put up on an old building site they stopped work at, up on the second floor of a half-finished car park or something. He showed me. It was so cool. He had everything there – even a little camping stove and a camping table and two chairs and everything. You got to hand it to him, Chris, he really knows how to do things properly.

We met in the park to look out for Billie, but she wasn't there. Then we caught the bus into Leeds. It was great. Me and a mate – just like the old days. Ruth was waiting for us at the bus station. She looked the pair of us up and down and smiled.

'Cool,' she said. 'So – let's meet the freaks.' And she led the way out of the station and on to the street.

I never realized about the Corn Exchange. There's

just a few people hanging about outside, but once you got round the back of it there were hundreds of them. Emos, punks, goths, gender-benders, mods, bikers, you name it. I didn't see any metalheads, though. I had on my new Metallica T-shirt that Mum got me in Manchester, but I had the original in my bag just to show anyone who wanted to see what a REAL T-shirt looked like. Even the new one usually stuck out a mile, but here it didn't make any difference. I actually looked normal.

Ruth didn't stick around long; she had her own freaks to hang out with. She pointed out where to go – around the back along the canal where people hung out. Chris and I went off on our own.

His eyes were falling out of his head.

'I've never seen so many freaks,' he kept muttering.

'No chavs, though,' I pointed out. 'They're the real freaks.'

Chris reckoned that since everyone else was there, there must be chavs too, so we started a chav count – and there were a few. But only the hardcore ones, the dressed-up ones, not the half-baked kind.

Put it like this – no Rileys.

Then we found them – the metalheads. There was a group of them, studded jackets, torn jeans, standing around drinking beers by the canal. One of them caught my eye – big bloke like me but a good foot taller than I was. He had long straight blond hair down to his waist and a denim waistcoat.

'It's Hell's Fairies,' breathed Chris in my ear. Then

the big bloke turned round and saw us. Maybe he heard. His eyebrows come beetling down. He stared me straight in the face. Then he handed his can to a mate and he came walking over to us, hair waving in the wind, glaring at me and my T-shirt. I thought, *No! Not again. Please. Can't I be here too?*

Chris

This bloke, he wasn't built like a brick shit-house, he *was* a brick shit-house. If you could make bricks out of muscles, he's what you'd have. There were quite a few fat bricks mixed up among the muscle bricks, but no one, no one, was ever going to tell this guy he was fat. As far as the rest of the world was concerned, he was Mr Slim. Big staring eyes rolling around in his head, hair down to his waist, beard – completely mad; you could tell that at once. He stuck out his belly, glared down at Rob's T-shirt and he bellowed –

'Metallica?'

Just our luck. A metalhead who hates Metallica. How many of them can there be?

And Rob, instead of begging for mercy or running or screaming or something sensible, sticks his belly right back out at the big bloke and shouts back. 'Yeah! Metallica!'

The man-mountain bloke bulged. His head swivelled on his fat neck. Veins stuck out like crocodiles.

'Metallica?' he bawled, spraying us both with bits of recently eaten people.

Rob didn't hesitate. 'Metallica!' he bawled back, stepping in so close he was almost wiping his nose on the monster's beard.

The monster swelled – I mean, literally, you could see him swelling. He swung his huge meaty fist in the air and waved it around under Rob's nose. 'Metallica!' he screamed epileptically. Vocab wasn't his thing, I guess.

'Yeah! Metallica!' bawled Rob back, and he yelled so loudly, right in his face, that his feet left the ground.

I was beginning to understand why he got bullied so badly at school. At this point Ruth came running over and I thought, *Oh, good, she can sort it out*. Even this monster wouldn't hit a girl. But evidently he would because as soon as she saw who it was she turned round and backed off rapidly into the crowd.

It was up to me.

'Hi, guys,' I dreebled. 'Yeah, Metallica, love 'em or hate 'em, eh? They're soooo like Marmite. We're all friends here, eh? Ha ha ha ha ha!'

I was going to have to rethink being Rob's mate after all. It was too life-threatening.

No one took any notice of me.

'Metallica!' bawled the big bloke.

'Metallica!' bawled Rob back.

'Metallica? Metallica?'

'Yeah! Metallica!'

'Fucking Metallica?'

'Yeah! Metallica!'

You get the picture. The other heavy-metallers lounged around by the rails shouting – you guessed it – 'Metallica!' from time to time. I was just thinking, *This is going on a bit*, when Rob stopped yelling and beamed at the monster.

'Mate!'

'Robbie!'

'Frankie!'

'Robbie! Mate!'

And they flung their arms round each other and did a big, huggy dance round one another. It wasn't aggression at all. It was heavy-metal man love.

It turned out they used to know one another years ago when they both lived in Manchester.

'This is Frankie,' rasped Rob. 'He's my mate. We used to play together.'

'Yeah . . . and look at you, man – you turned into a Metallica fan. How cool is that?'

'Yeah – and you! Amazing.'

'Yeah, man. In a band, man,' said Frankie, raising his eyebrows significantly.

'In a band? How cool is that?'

'Pretty cool, man, pretty cool.'

'What's it called?'

'You'll never guess, man.'

'No!'

'Yeah.'

'No!'

'Yeah, yeah. Kill All Enemies, man. KAE.'

'That's, like, our band!'

'Yeah. The real thing. Living the dream, man. Just getting going,' said Frankie. 'I'm the songwriter and I'm on rhythm, and this is Jamie – he plays a meeeean lead.'

'Drums?' asked Rob.

'To be appointed,' said Frankie.

And Rob, his face just fell. I never saw someone go from high to low so fast. A second ago he looked like he'd just discovered the secret of eternal life. Now, suddenly, he looked as if it involved eating a pound of shit a day.

It didn't take much working out. He meets up with his old mate. There's a band! It's the exact same band him and his mate used to dream about! Whoa! The band needs a drummer. Hey! Rob can drum. All he ever wanted was to be in a band. Perfect!

Except he has no drums.

He told me about his stepdad pinching them off him. How low can you get? I thought my parents were bad, but they'd never stoop that low. It made me wonder. Maybe my old pair weren't so bad after all.

You couldn't help feeling sorry for Rob, but I must admit my main feeling was one of relief. He told me all about his evil stepdad getting rid of his drum set a couple of days ago, and I was so outraged on his behalf that I almost told him about my drums, the eBay ones.

That was a narrow escape, eh? my brain said. *If you'd told him about those drums, you'd have to invite this band of hairy monsters round to our place to try them out.*

And at exactly the same moment, I heard my mouth going, 'Hi! I'm Chris's mouth and I just happen to have some drums at home that I never use.'

What? No – no! Stop! begged my brain. In silence, unfortunately.

'We could go there right now,' my mouth added. 'You can bring your instruments along and rehearse in my garage, if you like.'

It was bound to happen. My mouth had been going *blab blab blab guff guff guff* for years. So far, we'd got away with it. Now it comes out with this one stupid thing and everything unravels so fast I was on another planet in seconds.

Turned out Frankie had a van. Turned out they'd just been doing a gig at a youth project in a club round the corner, so they not only had a van with them – they had their instruments as well. How convenient.

The van was only ten minutes away. We set off at once.

There were only two of them actually in the band, but they all had to come, of course – all six of them. I can tell you, it was a weird sensation walking through the streets of Leeds with that lot. I mean, Frankie was enormous, but even the little ones were all dressed up in leathers, manky old jeans, badges, T-shirts covered in bad plastic pictures of motorbikes and road-kill. Long hair, dark glasses. It was like going for a stroll down the high street with a selection of Pleistocene mega-fauna. People quailed and stalled in the street as we approached. Body-builders, even big ones, stepped into the gutter and cringed as we passed.

My brain was furious with me. *What are you doing?* it was yelling inside my skull. *Aren't you in enough shit already? What happens when your parents find out? And how long anyway do you think it's gonna be before these freaks turn on you and break you up into little pieces? These people are ANIMALS! They're going to break into the house and destroy everything – the furniture, the fridge, the lot. Run now before it's too late!*

You know what brains are like. Always looking for the worst possible scenario.

Rob was off his head with excitement. He must have thought he'd died and gone to heaven. One minute he's Billy No Mates, the next he's walking along with a bunch of fellow monsters going to play in a band. He didn't know who to talk to first – me or Frankie or the other guys. So he just talked to us all at the same time instead.

On the way, we passed this woman, quite an old lady she was, packing a massive load of shopping into this car. The car was parked on the main road and her husband was sitting inside, nagging at her to get a move on before they got nicked. He kept leaning out of the window and shouting at her.

So Frankie holds up his hand, they all stop and, next

thing, they're helping her get the shopping in the boot. It was hilarious. The woman was standing there while the mega-fauna were passing the bags to each other going, 'Thanks, man. Hey, watch out for those crisps – they're going to get crushed under all that fruit you're putting on top.' And, 'Oh, Tropicana with the juicy bits. Good choice.' Surreal.

I was thinking, *Maybe I'm going to like this lot after all*.

The poor woman didn't know whether to be grateful or scared or just embarrassed. She stood there quivering, while her husband cringed behind the wheel, looking up and down the road and trying not to be there.

When they'd done, Frankie bends down to the window.

'If you don't mind me saying so,' he says to the hubby. 'I think your behaviour here was really pretty selfish, man.'

The man clutched the steering wheel and stared up at him. Frankie patted the lady on the head and off we went, snorting with laughter at the look on the old guy's face.

I'm, like, *Wow! How cool are these guys*.

You know what I think? I think brains aren't right nearly as often as they think they are.

The coast was clear as far as I knew. It was my nan's birthday that weekend and Mum and Dad were off to see her. The car was gone, but I left the lads outside while I went inside to double-check. Empty. I went into the garage, dug out the drums and opened up.

They all bundled in and started setting up the amps and the guitar. Rob got behind the drums and rattled away nervously. I was a bit embarrassed for him, because, be honest, he wasn't very good. Once the amps were going, Frankie came and did the guitar thing with Rob where you play to each other. Then they flung into a few chords – relief! They were ALL rubbish. Nothing to worry about. It was all crap together.

They faffed about a bit, tuning up. Then they launched into it. Apparently Rob was being crap in a wrong sort of way. Frankie took him over to where a big old mirror was leaning up against the wall and they both stood there, side by side, staring into the mirror, breathing deeply.

'What are they doing?' I asked the other guitarist.

'Frankie'll be visualizing one of his stepdads,' whispered Jamie reverentially. 'It's his pre-gig preparation. I expect he's getting Rob to do the same.'

It went on for about five minutes. They stood there side by side, breathing harder and harder, shoulders heaving, faces twisting up like some kind of Japanese B movie . . .

'YAAAAAAH!' screamed Frankie suddenly.

'GRAAAAAAAAAAAAAAAAAAAAAAAAH!' bawled Rob. They both dashed over to their instruments and started thrashing at them like they were tearing a dead cow apart limb from limb.

Energy! You know what? I began to get it. They couldn't play all that well, sure – but the energy was terrific. One of the other lads turned the volume up full and off they went.

Yea! Those guys were lifting the roof off. Ferocious. I sat and enjoyed the scenario, sipping a can of beer. I was feeling pretty good about things, I have to admit. I was the good guy. I'd got Billie off her charges – maybe even got her back in the Brant, once they found out where she was. I'd made friends with a lad I thought was a monster but who turned out to be a good mate, and I'd been able to give the mega-fauna a good time. Not bad for a week's work, when you think about it.

Gradually, I became aware of another noise in the background – a sort of soft, screaming gibber. It might have been a loud screaming gibber, actually, but it had no chance of getting itself heard above Kill All Enemies. Those guys were doing some seriously professional bawling and yelling. I turned round to see what it was and there was this red-faced dwarf jumping up and down and screeching and howling and waving its little fists in the air. It was horrible. It was barely human. It looked so . . . so out of place. Then it charged.

It was my dad.

I've never seen anyone so angry. He came rushing up to me so fast he practically knocked me over. He grabbed hold of me by the shirt front and started shaking me and shrieking. He was so close by now I could actually make out what he was shouting above the noise of the band.

'Who gave you permission to turn up with this lot!

Who gave you permission, who gave you the right! How dare you? GraaaAhhhhaaaah!'

His shouting got louder as the band died down until it was just him screaming. He ran out of words and stood there, clutching my shirt and panting hoarsely.

Frankie put down his guitar and came across.

'Man,' he said to my dad. 'You really need to do some work on that anger problem you have.'

'What? How dare you? Get out! Get out of my house!' He shoved his weight up against Frankie to try to shift him. He might as well have been pushing a house.

Frankie leaned across and whispered loudly to me, 'Who is it?'

'It's my dad.'

'What's wrong with him?'

'Dunno. He's always like this.'

'Get out, get out! Get out of my house or I'll call the police!' screamed my dad again. Of course he was pretty well unable to do anything against six blokes, all of them two or three times bigger than he was. All he could do was stand and shout while they all looked at him shaking their heads sadly.

'Is he safe?' asked Frankie.

'Yeah, harmless really,' I sighed. 'But you better go now anyway. Sorry,' I said.

Frankie sighed and turned to Dad. 'Since we've been asked *nicely*,' he said, 'we're going to leave now. But it would've made it a lot easier if you'd just been polite in the first place.'

'That's it. I'm calling the police,' he snarled.

'What for? Don't be daft! Excess politeness? We're going,' I said. I started to help the band pack up their stuff.

I was furious. Humiliated. The guys might look tough but they were nice people, while my dad, he looked nice enough but here he was behaving like a complete delinquent. Strange, eh? You know your parents all your life; you just take them for granted. You think they're decent people. And then one day something like this happens and you realize that, all along, they're just thugs.

'You – over here. Over here!' screamed my dad at me.

'Won't be a minute,' I said. 'I'm helping.'

'Gaaahhhhrrrrgh!' he howled. But there was nothing he could do so he stormed out. I helped the lads pack up. They were just leaving when Dad popped his head back in.

'And don't let me see you here again!' he bawled.

'Someone,' said Frankie, 'needs to have a little think about their manners, if you ask me.' He wagged his finger at my dad, who turned white with . . . I dunno, fear? Rage? The band said their goodbyes to me and turned to leave. I was about to follow on but Dad grabbed hold of me.

'You bastard,' he breathed. 'But I've got you now. I've bloody got you now, haven't I?'

He jerked his head to the house. We went inside and he began the whole miserable argument all over again from scratch. School, homework. All that. I just sat there and listened to him going on and on and on, thinking, *Do I really have to put up with this? Do I? I mean – really?*

Rob

Can you believe it? Yesterday I was nothing, and today look at me! I am in a band! Yeah, yeah – you heard. I am the official drummer in KAE.

'But I've got no drums,' I said.

'Drums will come, man,' Frankie said. 'You have to improvise. Sometimes the best music comes out of having to improvise. And stay angry! That's the main thing. That's your instrument, man – anger.'

That is so true. That is so, so true. It goes to show that even a tosspot like Philip can be useful for some things.

'This is my brother,' said Frankie to the other guys. 'And I christen him the Juggernaut, because nothing stops our kid here from going forward.'

Juggernaut – yeah! That's me.

It was the best day in my entire life.

And what about Chris? How cool is he – taking us round to let us play on his drums? I have so much respect for that guy. But now I understand why he doesn't want to live at home. Psychodad! It just shows – you can't ever tell. That man should be so proud of his son, and all he can do is shout and rage at him. What's wrong with the world? We were worried about him. Frankie drove round the block a few times while we tried to decide if we should go in and sort it out.

'Let us know if he comes into the Brant on Monday, see if he's got any bruises,' said Frankie in the end. He drove me back to my place and parked up, and we all swore an oath to be brothers together. Then I got out and the guys drove off. I walked up to the gate.

Philip's car was there. I touched the bonnet and it was warm. I thought, *He's been out*. I thought, *He's in there now, waiting for me*.

I opened the gate and walked up the garden to the front door. As I walked, I shrank. I started off nine feet tall at the gate but by the time I was fitting the key in the door I'd shrunk all the way down to the height of about your average piece of shit.

Billie

Cookie and me, we're two of a kind. All he thinks about is having a laugh and where his next drink's coming from. I can get that. He's the kind of bloke Hannah would say isn't good enough for me, but at least he doesn't try and tell me how I ought to be living my life. And he's willing to feed me and put me up. He gave me a key so I could let myself in and out, and a twenty to get some stuff in while he was out at work. Keep me out of sight while the police are looking for me. Who else is going to do that for me? Barbara and Hannah?

I don't think so. What are friends for? If you can't do that for me, don't bother.

Cookie was working afternoons and evenings, so he slept late, but we had a couple of hours the next morning after I turned up. It was good. I felt OK for the first time in ages. I was tempted to go back and pick up some spare clothes and get my phone from Barbara's. If I had the phone, maybe I'd have rung Hannah. But I didn't dare. The local cops all know my face. I'd be picked up in a minute.

I put my things in the washer. Cookie had Sky, so I watched a few old episodes of *Gavin & Stacey* and *Friends*, then I got bored so I started cleaning up the flat. Make myself useful. I can be proper domestic if I get the chance. I didn't have a change of clothes, though, and I looked a right idiot running around dressed in a pair of Cookie's boxers and a T-shirt. Still, by the time he came back about eight, I had it nice. He was pleased.

'Look at me, pissing in a clean pan. Like a king, I am. This is the life,' he was going.

And I was going, 'Get off, you moron,' but I was pleased too. I wasn't so pleased when his mate Jez turned up, with me in Cookie's underpants. I had to borrow a pair of trackie bottoms to cover up. I felt like an idiot. They thought it was hilarious, especially Jez. Then he kept trying it on, like he always does – brushing past and offering to give me one and trying to touch me up. He does it like it's a joke, right under Cookie's nose. Cookie just ignores him, but he doesn't like it. I can tell, the way he looks. He never dares say anything, though. He's always going on about how him and Jez are these big mates, but that's not being much of a mate. I reckon he's scared of him. He's a big bloke, Jez, and he gets funny when he doesn't get things his own way. Like I said, I don't do bullies. I said to Cookie ages ago, just pick a fight with him. Even if you lose, he won't come round any more. Get it over with. That's what I'd do. But it's not my house and it's not my mate, so I just have to put up with it.

That kind of put a spoiler on the night. They stayed

up for hours drinking. Cookie's about the most thoughtless bloke in the world – but he makes me laugh. He doesn't care about anything and I can't stay cross with him for long. He came to bed and we made up. He gave me some more money in the morning to go and buy some pants and stuff the next day, and some trackies that fitted, so at least I had a change of clothes.

I shouldn't have bothered cleaning the flat, though. It gave him ideas. He came home a few days later wanting his tea.

'What do you want tea for?' I asked him. 'You've been working in a restaurant all day.'

'I'm sick of burgers,' he said. 'I want some proper tea.'

'Get lost. I'll boil you an egg, then.'

'No, that's breakfast.'

'Like we're married? You must be joking. What do you want?'

'I dunno. Something that's not burgers and chips. Go on, Billie.'

'I can't cook.'

'You're a girl.'

'You noticed.'

'You do domestic science at school, don't you?'

'I don't go to school. I hate domestic science.'

'Go on. It's fair. You're staying here.'

'I'm not your mum.'

'I know. Go on.'

He drove me mad. I went out and bought him some ready meals in the end. He moaned about how much it cost, but he liked it. It was stupid, but it was kind of fun once I got over the idea. I looked forward to him coming home from work. It was nice to make him welcome. I made a deal with him, that I'd get some food in for him if he had a shower when he got back. He stank of burgers. The sofa stank of burgers where he'd been sitting on it, the bed stank of burgers, everywhere stank of burgers. I stank of burgers. I'd just wash my stuff and he'd come back and be all over me and I'd smell as bad as he did.

We got a nice little routine going after a while. He'd come home with something to drink, we'd open a can while I heated up his dinner. Then we'd eat, then I'd make him have a shower before he got anywhere near me. Then we'd watch a bit of telly.

'This is great. Clean house, dinner in the oven, sex on the table,' he said. 'This must be what people have girlfriends for.' He's a laugh. I didn't mind. One day a really nice fella'll come along, I suppose, but meanwhile, I dunno. I don't mind. Cookie's not the brightest candle on the cake, but at least you know what you're getting. He's on my side. He was putting me up and paying my way. I knew it wasn't going to last forever but for now, for a couple of weeks or something . . . it was OK.

Chris

'We made a deal with you, Chris,' said my mother. 'We dropped the charges against that girl on condition that you went to school.'

'That wasn't a deal, that was blackmail,' I pointed out.

'You lied to us,' she seethed.

'I'm sorry? You, a blackmailer, are trying to take the moral high ground here? I don't think so.'

'Chris . . .'

'Do you realize that Billie's been missing for over a week now? That's how worried she is, and you were prepared to put her whole future at risk just because you want me to fall in with *your* plans for *my* future. What are you people on?'

'Right, that's it. I'm going to hit him now,' said my dad. You see how these types turn to violence when they can't get what they want through negotiation.

My mother restrained him, but rather half-heartedly, I thought. Dad launched off on this huge list of prohibitions and no-nos and various other denials of my basic human rights. Stopping my money *for the rest of the year*, for instance (!!!???!). Or until I caught up on my homework. Mum had no problem with that. She couldn't agree more with that. But how about removing all my best clothes from the cupboard . . . ?

'Why?' she wanted to know.

'So he's encouraged not to go out any more,' said my dad.

'I can go out without trousers if necessary,' I told them.

Dad looked at me and frowned. 'Would he?' he asked Mum.

'He might,' she replied.

She overruled him on that one. But then this: removing my drums and giving them to charity in order to make sure there were no more unauthorized guests coming round to play them.

She concurred with that without so much as a blink.

'You're going to take my property away from me?' I asked them mildly. 'That's what's usually known . . . now what's the word, it's on the tip of my tongue . . . ah yes! Theft, isn't it?'

'It's not theft: you're not sixteen – we're your parents,' snipped my mother.

'Yeah, you're not old enough to own anything, really,' said my father.

I didn't even bother replying. I simply made up my mind, very quietly and without informing them, that none of the above was going to happen.

*

So. Monday morning. I went about my business. School. Work. Wikes. After spending days away from it, it was even worse. The Chris Trent bored-ometer was tested to its limits.

I suffered it all without complaint.

'What are you up to?' said my mum at the end of the first day.

'Nothing. I've decided to give up,' I said.

'It won't work,' said my dad.

Part one of the plan was under way – lulling them into a sense of security. False, of course. Tuesday, more of the same. By Wednesday, they were both sufficiently lulled to go out. They thought they were safe because school was over. They were wrong.

Mum was out with a friend, Dad was off doing a training course to try and improve his interview skills. Alex's brother had a van. Perfect.

I had to explain the whole thing very carefully to Alex. For some reason, he seemed to think he had some sort of a responsibility to tell his brother what was actually going on.

'John doesn't *want* to know what's going on,' I pointed out. 'If he knows what's going on, he might have to say no and then he'd have to do without the money which he very sorely needs. Correct?'

'But it's theft!'

I might have been a little bitter at that point. You know how it is. You make friends in infant school when you don't know what's what, then by the time you grow up enough to make sense of things you realize you've befriended a pig's pizzle in a monkey suit, and it's too late to do anything about it.

'We've already gone through this,' I breathed to Alex. 'You can't steal your own things. Ergo, it's not theft.'

'But you're still a minor. Everything you own belongs to your mum and dad. Technically, you don't own anything. Ergo, it is theft.'

The politics of cowardice. I should have learned by now. Me and Alex – it's just history repeating itself, really. In the end, we made a deal. I needed access to his brother John and for Alex to keep quiet about the lack of parental cooperation in the matter. He needed me not to tell his mum about how he used to borrow her underwear for embarrassing purposes.

'You wouldn't do that.'

'Wouldn't I?'

'Anyway, I was only looking.'

'She doesn't know that.'

Yes, I know he was only eleven at the time, but, believe me, the embarrassment value had only grown over the years.

It all went smoothly – right up to the end when Mum came back early. Her timing was immaculate. We had the kit loaded on to the van and John had just started the engine when she turned up in her Mini. Two more minutes and we would have got clean away, but instead I had to sit there and watch her drive up and pull over next to us.

I wound down my window.

'What are you doing?' she asked curiously.

I could see John looking anxiously over at me. The situation could go critical at any moment. I decided to go for broke. I leaned down and talked quietly to her.

'I wouldn't tell Dad if I was you. You know how stressed he gets. If he thinks it's me, he'll go round the twist. He has enough on his plate already.'

'Chris, what are you talking about?'

I left the awful scenario to her imagination and turned to John. 'Let's go,' I said.

'That's your mum, isn't it?' said John. 'Why's she looking at you like that?'

'Because she's my mum,' I answered, more or less truthfully.

John didn't look happy, but he waved to her, put the van into gear and we drove off. She just sat there and watched. Her expression was unreadable. I think I saw her cast a suspicious glance at the garage as we headed off down the road, but by that time it was too late. Even so, I turned off my mobile. Just in case.

Later on, when Dad came home and discovered that some bastard had come in and nicked my drums, he was utterly and totally enraged out of all proportion. I pointed out to him that the unknown thief had only done what he had been planning to do himself, so what was his problem? And – can you believe this? – he actually found it in his black heart to blame me. I was furious. I mean, he didn't *know* that, did he? It was sheer bias. He got so angry about it he punched the wall, really hard, and made a mess of his hand. Mum just looked at me, but she never said a word about it to him as far as I know.

But that was for later. As I sat in the van and sped off into town, I was feeling on top of the world. I had achieved the impossible. I had stolen my own possessions.

Rob

We were in the hall in the Youth Centre rehearsing. I was on tambourine and it was making me so angry. There I was, in the middle of a fantastic heavy-metal band. I could have been the drummer, but instead – I was on heavy-metal tambourine.

And it was all that prick Philip's fault.

It was like pure, unadulterated hatred and I was thinking, *It's wrong, feeling like this.* It means he's won. Philip has turned me into a hateful little toad just like him. Can you imagine that? Being turned into the thing you hate the most on this earth. That's what monsters do to you. They don't eat you – they turn you into one of them.

Then this bloke turned up. I'd never seen him before. We all just stared at him, like, you know, who did he think he was, walking into our rehearsal without even knocking.

'Rob Crier?' he asked.

'What?' I said. I thought it was trouble.

He nodded behind him. 'Delivery for you.'

'It can't be me.'

'It's for you all right. Out here.' The guy turned and went out, and we all trooped after him.

Get this.

There's a van backed up close to the door.

There's Chris standing next to the van.

'What's going on?' I asked.

The other bloke flung open the van doors and Chris goes, 'Da da!'

It was the drums.

'They're yours,' he said.

'What?'

'They're yours!'

'What?' I just stood there and stared. It wasn't sinking in.

'You talked your dad round?'

'No. I'm giving them to you. Happy birthday.'

'It's not my birthday.'

'Roly, I'm giving you the drums. Do you want them or not?'

I stood there like a complete idiot. Everyone was looking at me waiting to see what I was going to say.

'Why would you . . .' I began, but I had to stop.

'I don't need them,' said Chris. 'You might as well have them.'

Then Frankie suddenly yelled out, 'We have drums! We've got a drummer! We're a fucking band!' And everyone was running about punching the air and hugging each other and shouting like maniacs.

I was so gobsmacked I couldn't move. I was still just

stood there . . . Frankie went up to Chris and gave him a big hug. He said, 'Total, total respect, for what you've done for Rob and us as well. Total. Total. Respect.'

'No prob,' said Chris.

Then all the other lads crowded around him making a fuss, and I still hadn't said a word. So I walked up and I pushed them out of the way, and I put my arms round him and I hugged him and I hugged him until my voice came back, and then I pulled back and I pointed at the tears that were on my face, and I said, 'This is the only way I can show you how you've made me feel.' Which was pretty wet, but I didn't care. I didn't care about anything. I couldn't talk for a bit again after that, but when my voice came back, I took the biggest breath I ever took in my life and went – 'YA-HAAAAAAAAA AAAAAAAAAAAAAAAAAAAAAAAY!'

Chris

Once in a while, just once in a while, you can make someone's dreams come true. It isn't even always that hard.

Suddenly, because of me, Kill All Enemies was a proper band, so of course they wanted to celebrate it by playing, a good old thrash, with a full drum kit. There was this big scramble to set it all up. Rob spent some quality time kissing them – at least it wasn't me this time. Then he sat down and did a quick roll. Then Frankie, the big bloke, gave out this terrible guttural croak, and off they went.

Bum notes, jangled chords, mis-struck strings – it had them all. But the noise. I'd forgotten just how much noise they made. Every time I heard them, it took my breath away. They were howling and gnashing their teeth and beating up their kit like it had just spat on their girlfriends.

They got to the end of the first track. They stopped. Frankie turned round to look at me, his eyes as wide as saucers.

'Awesome,' he said.

'Amazing,' said another one.

'We are FANTASTIC!' yelled Frankie. And Rob started crying again – he does a lot of that – and they all started dancing around and high-fiving, like they'd just won the lottery.

Off they went into more songs. It was great. They did three and that was it. They didn't have any more songs. Just the three. Then we had biscuits and things. The lads kept stopping and gazing wetly into the distance, and then turning round and saying . . .

'Respect, man.'

'No problem.'

'Total respect.'

'What did your dad say?' someone asked.

'He said he was glad to get rid of them,' I told them. No point in diluting my sainthood by pointing out to them it was also an act of petty vengeance, was there? I was just thinking of leaving them to it, when suddenly Frankie had this big announcement.

'Listen, Chris, mate,' he said. 'We've got something to say.' All the band were standing around looking at me and smiling shyly. It was obviously the big thank-you. I prepared myself for more manly hugs and tears.

'We've been talking about it,' said Frankie. 'All of us, we're agreed. What you've done, man, it's amazing. Truly awesome. You are the man. You're one of us. And the thing is, I can see you know how to get things done. I can see you like the sound. So the thing is – we want you to be a part of it.'

I was about to object, but he waved me quiet.

'I know you don't play. I know you're not into metal as such. That doesn't matter. We play. Chris, what we want to ask you is – will you be our manager?'

My jaw just dropped. Manager? Me? Is this what happens when you do people favours? They want to own you for the rest of your life, doing them more favours? I couldn't believe it. I was standing there thinking, What? Manage your band? You must be joking. I'd rather give birth to a wolverine than manage your band.

My brain was shouting at me: *No way! Tell them to go away, tell them your mum is paralysed from the waist down, tell them you can't add up – anything! Just say no. NO! NO! NO!*

And my mouth said, 'I'd be honoured, man.'

NOOOOOOOOOOOOOO! howled my brain.

'Really. It's great. I'd love to,' said my mouth. And they all started whooping and hugging and crying, and the odd thing was, I was whooping and hugging and crying along with them. Weird. It was, like, I know nothing. I'm not even the same person I thought I was.

One of the lads went out and bought loads of beer and someone had some weed, and we had a party. The band played – even I played and I can't play. As I got drunker I stopped listening to all the duff notes and the jangly chords and stuff, and I started to listen to the *sound*. So they aren't much good yet – so what? They can learn. I bet Oasis weren't much good when they started out. I bet their parents hated the noise they made. Or Beethoven. I bet when Beethoven started playing the piano his mum said to him, 'Ludwig, give it up – you're deaf.'

Anyone can get good. You just have to practise. KAE had something else: energy. They were real. They were like a thousand tons of rock coming down the mountain straight for you. It made your hair stand on end . . . once you'd had a few drinks.

Maybe, I thought, *just maybe, this could actually work*.

It wasn't till ages later, when I was on my way home, that I suddenly thought, *You know what? I've got a job. More than that – I've actually got something I want to do*. I never thought about it before, but my whole life up till then was just practice. Even eBay. I was just spending my time avoiding the things I didn't want to do and filling up the spaces with football and hanging out and . . . games. But this was real. I belonged to something. Those guys knew who I was and what I was about. They got it. When they said, 'Respect,' they meant it. OK, so they were hairy and covered in studs, and I wore trainers and sports gear, but I was already more like them than I ever would be like Alex. Or Dad. Or anyone else I knew.

Respect.

I thought, *I'm not going to be able to find time for school now, even if I wanted to*.

Billie

It was a Saturday night. I'd been there for ages, over a week. It was working out. Cookie was on lates that night – the place where he works stays open till about twelve on a Friday and Saturday. I was looking forward to it. A night on me own, in front of the telly. I had a bath, a good old soak, found myself a film, settled down . . . there's a key in the door. Well, who's that? Only bloody Jez and a couple of his mates.

'Cookie's out,' I told them.

'Is he? We bought some booze and stuff,' said Jez.

'No, he's not here. I was going to have a night in.'

'He won't mind,' said Jez. In they all came. I could have cried. They knew bloody well he wasn't there. Spending the night with Jez and his creepy mates was the last thing I wanted, but there was nothing I could do about it. We all knew, if I rang Cookie and asked him, he'd back Jez up. He always does. Cookie gave him a key ages ago. He doesn't even live here, what's he got a key for? It's stupid. He just does whatever Jez tells him. It drives me mental.

There were three or four of them – Jez, this lad called Staffs, and a couple of others. There was nothing for it. They were going to be there all night now. They'd wait up for Cookie until he got back and then he'd want some. I was going to be up all night out of my head with a bunch of losers.

I went on the voddie and orange, but I was taking it easy. I didn't want to lose it with this lot around. It tasted a bit strong so I sneaked out and poured a bit away and watered it down. Then, a bit later, I put the glass on a stack of CDs and spilt it all down the CDs. Cookie would have gone bonkers – he loves his music – so I wiped it up with my sleeve and went into the kitchen to get another without telling anyone. I'd only had about half.

And then, then I was on my way back into the front room, and I was staggering. You know? Like, out of it already. I was thinking, *What's up with me?* I hadn't had anything, just half of one voddie, so what was I doing staggering?

'I'm going already,' I said to Staffs, who was behind me.

'Aye, he mixes them strong, Jez,' said Staffs, and he gave me this look, this funny look.

We sat around listening to music and talking a bit. I remember getting up to look for a CD and the way they all laughed when I lurched across the room. I was falling down. I went back to park myself on the sofa, but . . . I hadn't even finished one drink. How could I be so drunk already?

Then it went blurry. I was on the sofa snogging Jez. I don't know how it happened. Then suddenly it wasn't Jez, it was Staffs, and then he was feeling me up. And someone was fiddling with my top and trying to get their hand down my pants, and . . .

I sat up and pushed them off and I was thinking, *This is wrong. I don't do that. I'm with Cookie.* I might be rubbish, but I'm not getting shared out like a pack of jelly beans. And I'd only drunk a little bit . . . and all the other blokes were in the room as well, watching it . . .

I started to panic then, because I was so out of it there was nothing I could do. That's how it felt – like there was nothing I could do about it. I got up and went to the loo, not that I needed to go, but I wanted some head space. I got in there and splashed some water on my face, trying to wake up. I was so out of it. I sat down, and I was thinking, *This is wrong, this is all wrong, I'm not that drunk, I can't be.*

And of course, at the back of my head, I knew what it was already. I'd been spiked, hadn't I? I'd been spiked, and that shit Jez and his useless mates were going to take turns with me.

I was the night's entertainment.

I was thinking, *This can't be true, this can't be happening to me. This isn't how you get raped. You get held down and you shout and you scream, and you fight. You get beat up. You don't just lie back on the settee and watch it happen to you. You don't go to bed and forget about it overnight.*

Sod this.

I stood up, tried the window. It was open, but I

couldn't climb out. I just couldn't do it. I couldn't get my leg up high enough. I kept falling down. I staggered out of the loo and into the passage, trying to keep quiet. The living-room door was closed and there was music and laughter going on in there, but I still had enough sense not to go down the hall in case I banged about and they heard me. I turned round and went into the kitchen at the back. Back door, locked. I didn't realize at first. I just tugged, then I wasted more time trying to find the key, but it was a bolt all the time. Then I wasted more time fumbling with that . . .

The bastard, he must have been watching me for ages. I'd just eased the door open when an arm shot out and banged it shut.

Jez.

'Not leaving the party, Billie?' he said.

'I wanna go,' I said, trying to push him out of the way.

'Not yet,' he told me. He flicked the bolt back across. I watched stupidly. I just couldn't move at any speed at all. Then he took my arm and started to lead me back into the living room. My feet just patted along like a good girl doing as she was told. And the thing was I almost didn't care. Almost. I almost could have let him lead me back into the living room so I could get raped. Who knows – I might not even remember it, so who cared . . .

But I did care. I wedged my arms against the living-room door.

'Kitchen,' I muttered. 'Left it in there . . .'

'What?' he asked.

'. . . Moment . . .' I said, and pushed my way back. And the bastard, he let me get all the way to the back door, and he let me faff around and undo the bolt and start to open it again before he came up behind. I heard him coming, I tried to hurry, but I couldn't.

Then he jammed his hand down on the door and shut it hard again.

I turned to look up at him. And he looked at me and I looked at him. And he knew. He knew I knew and I knew he knew.

'Didn't finish your drink, did you?' he asked me.

'. . . Spiked me drink,' I said.

He shook his head. As if. He'd never admit it. He was too much of a coward. We stood there looking at each other a moment. Behind us there was a bell at the front door. He glanced over his shoulder at it.

'Couple more mates,' he told me, and he raised his eyebrow and winked.

'No,' I said. 'Don't,' I said. 'Please don't, Jez.'

He shook his head again. He stood back. 'Come on, love. It's OK.'

'It's not OK!'

He shook his head again. 'Come on, Billie,' he said. 'You never minded before . . .'

'I never knew before,' I said, but even as I was speaking I thought, *Before? This has happened before?*

Jez was watching me, smiling. He nodded. 'You liked it, Billie. You loved it. I watched you. I watched you enjoying it all night.'

I was trying to think . . . It was Rohypnol or something, wasn't it? Date rape. You don't know, you don't even remember it the next day. And he was saying it had happened before?

'You lying bastard,' I said. 'I don't believe you. I'd know. I'd've been sick for days just from touching you. Now let me go . . .'

I tried to push him away, but he just stood there. I was so weak I could hardly move myself, let alone him.

'What about Cookie? He's supposed to be your mate,' I said.

Jez sort of looked to one side and shook his head. 'Cookie don't mind, Billie. He don't mind sharing his things with his mates.'

'I'm not his thing . . .'

I tried to push him out of the way, but his arm on the door was like a tree – I couldn't budge it.

'Cookie wouldn't do this to me,' I said, and I started to cry.

'Never mind Cookie.'

Staffs had got to the front door by this time and let them in. Voices in the hall. Music. It all sounded underwater, but sort of normal. But it wasn't normal. It was way off being normal. I turned back to the door, but there was his arm, leaning down hard.

Jez bent down close to me. 'Think you're so tough, don't you?' he said. 'But you're not at the moment, are you, Billie? Not tough at all.' He shook his head. Then he smiled. 'Anyways, you might as well. Have another drink. You won't remember it. I'll keep an eye on things, make sure no one's too rough. Come on. Be a sport, Billie. What's wrong with you, love?' He took his arm out of the way and nodded at the door.

I stayed where I was.

'Money,' I said.

Jez rolled his eyes. Like, you know – why should I pay when I can get it for free?

'How much?' he asked. He put his hand to his pocket and leaned back.

I knew I was only going to get one go at it. I was lining him up, trying not to look at his crotch, taking my time, lining it up. I waited until he glanced down at his hand – then I launched my foot like a rocket.

It was perfect. He sank down without a noise like a sheet of wet newspaper. I turned round. It was all in slow motion. I fumbled at the door. It was just a bolt, but I couldn't get it. I could hear the other lads coming down the hall. He must have made more noise than I thought. Then I realized why it wasn't working – it was already open. He'd just slammed it shut. I yanked the door open, tumbled into the yard and slammed it behind me. Ran across the yard. Crawled on to a wall between his and his neighbour's yard. The door opened and they all burst out.

I lay on the wall for a moment. I looked at them; they looked at me. Then I rolled over and fell down hard to the ground on the other side. It was all I could do. Then I just lay there and waited.

'Shit,' someone said.

There was a pause. 'Bloody hell, Jez, now what?'

someone said. I guess they didn't know that I'd actually collapsed into a heap on the other side of the wall. Or they were worried about what the neighbours would think if they got caught dragging a half-conscious girl doped up on Rohypnol about. Either way, they stood about, muttering and complaining . . . then they went back in and closed the door behind them.

I waited a little bit in case one of them had stayed outside. Then I got up and clambered around the yard, banging about. I heard someone inside – an old lady, I think, calling out, 'Who's that?'

I took no notice. I got out over her wall, then another. I didn't want to get out into the alley behind the house in case they were waiting there for me. I got into another yard and waited there, just hid and waited there for hours. It felt like hours. Then I got out into the road. I staggered off till I found a hedge. I collapsed under the hedge. Closed my eyes. And passed out.

Hannah

They didn't look very happy. You can't blame them. Your child has been booted out of school, and then you get asked into the PRU for a little chat. Not just any PRU either – the PRU where your son has had his balls squashed. Not good news. And he's not even attending here any more.

But they came. Middle class, decent income. Do anything for their child. You don't get many like that here. You get a lot of poor kids – their kind of deprivation speaks for itself. Then you get the rich kids. Parents so busy they don't have time for them. It's a different sort of neglect, when you can have everything money can buy. But you know what the song says – 'Money Can't Buy Me Love'. Well, guess what? It can't. But, on the whole, middle-class parents tend to bring up their kids pretty well.

'It's good of you both to come. I know you don't have to.'

'Anything that might help Chris.' That was Dad.

'We'll be honest with you, though, Mrs –'

'Hannah. Call me Hannah.'

Mum. A social worker. She was used to working out the problems people have, not being told. If I had anything new to say, it was going to hit her right in her pride.

'We've been through pretty well everything there is to go through with Chris already,' she said.

'Well, I'll get straight to the point, then. So if I'm just going over old ground, I won't be wasting any more of your time. Basically, I think Chris has two issues to deal with.' They looked up. Surprised. That word – issues. They'd thought they were beyond that.

'He's a very stubborn boy,' said Dad. He paused. 'Go on, then,' he said.

'We know Chris is a bright boy – very bright,' I said. Start with the easy bit. 'I know Reedon is a grammar, but it's not a terribly good one. To tell you the truth, we don't have many dealings with it, but the reputation is it's seen better days. Not all that good at picking up on problems . . .'

'Both the school and us have been on Chris's case since he started there,' said Mum.

'Yes, well, I know the options for schools round your way aren't all that great. But the point is I don't think the school challenges Chris enough. He gets bored. As I say, very bright boy. Highly intelligent. Added to which – well. Just a little dyslexia.'

Pause.

I raised my eyebrows and smiled slightly. I tried not to look patronizing, nervous, amused or smug. They were both staring at me as if I'd just told them that Chris was a mermaid.

'Chris doesn't have dyslexia,' said Mum. 'He did tests for all that ages ago.'

'Did he? Where did he do them?' I asked.

'At school.'

'They were all negative,' said Dad.

'Not like these, then,' I said, and I whipped out the papers I got him to do.

They looked shocked. Her especially. Social worker, son at fifteen years with undiagnosed dyslexia? Not great.

I rattled through the evidence as they looked over the tests. Avoidance of any sort of reading and writing. Highly intelligent yet slow to produce written work. Forever finding ways of putting it off . . .

'Look at this. Look at this,' said Mum suddenly. She seized her handbag and wrenched it open, producing a beautifully written piece of work. Science.

'Chris did this the other day when we made him stay in. Look at it. This is good work. No spelling mistakes. Argument, evidence, conclusion. Perfect. Are you seriously telling me this is the work of a dyslexic?'

I looked it over. 'It's beautiful, but it's only one page long. Work at GCSE level should be far longer than that. As for perfect – well, that's a giveaway, isn't it? His website is the same. It's perfect, but he won't write a word in front of anyone. How come? Because he needs to spend hours checking it up and making sure it's exactly right. That's why no one ever sees Chris write.'

'But the tests he did at school,' said Dad. 'When did he do them?' he asked his wife.

'Year Eight.'

'He came through it with flying colours. What about that? You can't develop dyslexia, can you?'

I pulled a face. 'Chris has his techniques. He might have got a friend to do them for him. He might have smuggled them out and done them at his leisure . . .'

'That's ridiculous,' said Mum.

'Is it?' said Dad. 'After we've seen the lengths he'll go to? Is it?'

'How did you get him to do them, then?' demanded Mum.

'I sat next to him,' I said. I laughed. 'Poor Chris, I thought he was going to walk. He hated it so much.'

Mum had gone grey. Dad reached across and took her hand. Nice man. Where was the snorting imbecile Chris had told me about? You know what I thought to myself? You can't believe a single word that kid tells you. Not one.

'I can't believe . . .' she began. 'Are these tests right? Because if they are . . . I can't believe everyone's missed this.' She stopped and glanced suddenly at me. I knew what she was thinking.

Yes, love. And if you'd spent more time using your skills to observe your child instead of being so busy at work, you might have spotted it for yourself. And as a result he's one year away from his exams and he's lost the will to even try . . .

But I didn't say that of course. 'Mrs Trent,' I said.

'Chris is about the cleverest and certainly the most determined young man I think I've ever come across. He's been pulling the wool over everyone's eyes for years. It's not like there's a single problem. Any one of them – high intelligence, poor school, a little dyslexia – it wouldn't have mattered. Two of them – probably OK. Three of them – well . . . And let's not forget how determined Chris is. And how highly motivated. Very competitive too. He doesn't like doing things poorly, does he?' I shrugged. 'There you go.'

'I can't believe it.' She stared at the papers. 'The little bastard. The sneaky little bastard. All this time.'

I laughed. 'Be honest, though, Mrs Trent. You've got to admire him. And I'll tell you what. Chris is the one child who's going to make his way in the world whether he passes any exams or not.'

She tried to laugh, a bit shaky still. He smiled. They'd taken it. Fair play to them. That could not have been easy.

We spent a few minutes chatting about the Brant and the work we do and so on. I felt for her. If it had been her giving him those tests, she'd have done it properly. But it never occurred to her to question the school. Why would she?

By the time they left, they'd cheered up. Dad was positively skipping. 'At least we know what we're dealing with now,' he said.

Mum looked sideways at him.

'What?' he said.

'We've left it too late.'

‘It’s never too late,’ said Dad.

Then they left, clutching the papers. My feeling was she was right. It was too late, for GCSEs anyway. Well, good luck to them. I went back to my desk, picked up my phone and checked for messages. Still nothing from Billie. It’s been over a week now. Every day I get more convinced something awful’s happened. A message from Barbara. One word. ‘Nothing.’ Nothing nothing nothing. Come on, Billie – ring! Talk to me. Just talk. For God’s sake – at least let me know you’re still alive!

I tapped out another text. At least when she picks them up she’ll know how hard I’ve been trying. I’ve been doing about one an hour for the past week.

Billie, I love you. Get in touch. Hxxxx

Billie

I don't know what time it was when I woke up. Middle of the night. Freezing cold, pitch black. I got up and tried to move about. I was still staggering, but whatever they spiked me with was wearing off.

I started walking.

I had no idea what the time was but it got lighter as I walked. It took hours. All the time I was thinking, *You bastards, you bastards*. I'd never even have found out what they were going to do if I hadn't spilled that drink. And what he'd said about Cookie? 'He doesn't mind sharing his things with his mates.' All the times they'd come round and I'd got so drunk I didn't know what was going on. How many times?

I don't know if it's true. Jez is such a nasty bastard, he'd just say that. Cookie's scared of him. He wouldn't though. He never would. Would he?

I didn't even know if I'd already been raped.

I walked and I walked. I walked it off, the drug, whatever it was. At last the park came up. I saw one of the neighbours walking her dog. She called out, but I didn't answer. I just wanted to go home but it was still too early. I'd left my key at Cookie's. Barbara always locks the house up like a safe at night, so I sat down on a bench for a bit and I think I must have dozed.

Then I went home.

There was no one in.

I could have cried. If they'd been in, it'd be over. The LOK, Secure, back in the cells. But at least it'd be over. I wanted to sit down in a chair and wait for it, but as soon as I realized the house was empty I knew what I was going to do. I was going to steal as much money as I could get my hands on and go out on the run again. I had another few days of freedom. Nowhere to go, no one to see, nothing to do. But I was going to do it anyway.

I ran round the house and got in at the back. My phone was lying there on the table. Barbara had put some credit on it, wonders will never cease. I turned it on. Grabbed some clothes, stuffed them in a bag. I dug about in the drawers and found some money – not a lot, just a few quid. I thought I'd better raid the kitchen. There's sometimes a few quid hanging around in there and I needed food. I went in and looked in the cupboards and suddenly I found myself looking at the knives.

Cook's knives, I thought.

It stopped me in my tracks. And I felt sick that I'd thought of it because I knew I was going to have to do it. I was going down. God knows what else was coming my way, because, let's face it, I was losing it, wasn't I?

Anyone could see I was not doing well. And him, Jez – he was going to get away with it. With rape. Gang rape, him and his mates. They didn't have to worry about a thing.

And what about Cookie? Didn't you mind, Cookie? Didn't you care? Was this your way of helping out your mate who doesn't get any shags?

I don't know if he was lying about Cookie or not. I reckon he was lying. Either way, I was never going round there again. But Jez, he needed to suffer for what he'd tried to do to me.

Barbara keeps her knives in this knife block, about five or six of them together. I took out the biggest, this dirty big thing, blade like a sword, but then I remembered what someone said to me years ago when I was small. You use a thin blade to stab someone. Something long and thin that you can stick in and pull out fast. You don't want it getting stuck. In and out. And on the way out, you twist.

I put the big one down and took out a smaller one. Shorter, nice thin blade. Easier to conceal. Barbara has this little device in the drawer she uses to sharpen her knives with. I dug in the drawer and found it. It was like two little crossed arms. I ran the blade through it a few times and tested it on my thumb.

It'd do.

That's what got him off, did it, doing it to an unconscious girl and watching his mates take turns after him? And she never knows a thing about it? See how sexy he feels with this jammed in his insides.

I thought, *I'm going to do this. I've got nothing to lose; I've already lost everything. I can at least make sure he never does it to anyone else.*

I slid the knife into my bag and opened up the fridge. There was a note there, right in my face, saying – 'There's a note for you on the kitchen table.'

I looked behind me. It had been there all the time, but I'd never noticed it. First thing – there's a twenty-pound note folded inside the paper. What's that? Barbara never gives me money when I'm not behaving myself. I picked it up and I was about to read it through. I was just thinking that Hannah must have told her to leave me some cash, when I heard their voices outside. All of them. Barbara and Hannah and Dan, all of them together.

Jesus. They'd teamed up. That's all I needed.

I stuffed the note and money in my pocket and I legged it out the back door and up the garden. Glanced back – no one there yet. I scrambled over the fence – it was all overgrown; I got scratched to bits – ran through the garden at the other end and out on to the road.

As soon as I got clear, I ducked into the park to hide and have a read of that note – and you know what? I'd only gone and lost it. It must have fallen out of my back pocket when I was getting out. I couldn't believe it. And the money – twenty quid, gone! I went back to have a look for it, retraced my steps. And I found it too. Well, I saw it, anyhow – in the garden, about halfway down. It must have fallen out while I was running.

I was more upset about the note than the money. I suppose a bit of me must have wanted to know what they were going to say, even though I could guess it. I hid in the bushes at the back for about fifteen minutes until bloody Barbara came out and found it. She ran back into the house, going 'Hannah!' at the top of her voice.

So that was that gone, money and note, the lot. I went back down the park. I heard them shouting for me. No way. I had business to do.

I thought, *It's still early. Jez'd still be in bed.*

He worked evenings too, serving in a bar. I know where – Cookie and me'd been in there a few times. He'd said he was on at six. I remembered that much.

I'd take him out on his way to work. I didn't care if he died. He deserved to die. I'd get put away. Life. What's life? Twenty, maybe twenty-five years? Or maybe they'd drop some off because Jez is such a bastard. Then I'd only get twelve or even ten. Or maybe I wouldn't kill him. Maybe I'd just stick him and he'd lose a lot of blood and it'd be touch and go, but he'd live, and I'd get done for GBH instead. Or even, if I was lucky, no one would see me and I could do a runner and he'd die in a pool of blood and no one would even know who'd done it. That was the dream ticket. I wasn't counting on it, though, not with my luck. I was only going to get one chance at him, and I was going to make sure I took it. If I had to do it in the middle of the street with half of Leeds watching, I'd still do it.

I worked it all out in my head. I knew where he

lived. I'd get him on his way out of his flat. It was perfect. I could hide behind the bins – *bam!* In and out. The blade wasn't that long, but it was enough. At least I wouldn't have just taken it lying down, would I?

For once in my life I'd have done something good.

I patted my pocket for my phone. I thought I'd check my messages. Would you believe I'd left that behind as well? I could see it in my mind lying there on the kitchen table. They'd come back like that and I'd dashed out – stupid! Well, I wasn't going back to get it, was I? Not now.

Couple of hours to wait. Nothing to do. I found my old bench, tucked away where I wouldn't be spotted, and I waited. All I wanted was to be left alone, let the time pass, so I could do what I had to do. Then they could take me away and watch my life disappear down the plughole, like it was always going to.

Chris

Sunday morning. Band rehearsal. That's how I spend my weekends and evenings these days. We're using someone's garage at the mo. It's not great, but it's better than nothing.

The boys launched into a mighty rendition of 'Not My Daddy' – one of Frankie's better numbers. It was about your dad being an arsehole. I could relate to that. Things had been moving on. They had two in the band when they met me. Rob made three; now we had Jamie 2 on bass guitar. Four. Hang on, I hear you say – I thought the band didn't have a bass guitar to their name? Well, they did now. What's more it was a *free* bass guitar. The previous owner might have disagreed about the actual free-ness of it, but since my dad hadn't played it for at least a year – well, we could worry about that one later, couldn't we?

There was still a long way to go, mind. We needed better rehearsal space, more instruments, sound equipment. We needed more work on the line-up. Frankie was pretty impressive up there, but a bit . . . I dunno, it needed something more. I already had a couple of leads for another singer.

See? Manager. This is *so* much cooler than eBay. Talking to girls . . . 'Yeah, the manager. Book the gigs, try and give them a direction. You know. Working on a recording contract for the boys right now . . .'

The rehearsal went pretty well. I was actually discussing with the guys my plans for the line-up. I wanted them to consider a girl. Why not? There's a girl singer in Arch Enemy, which is one of their favourite bands. Check it out – it's a hot band. She's fantastic. With the right singer it adds, you know, interest.

Suddenly Rob jumped to his feet, phone in hand. 'They found her!' he shouted. 'Billie! They found her!'

'Where?'

'The park. I just had a text from Hannah. We have to go and help.'

It turns out that they hadn't actually found her yet. One of her neighbours saw her in the park. Hannah and her carer and God knows who else went rushing round to grab her – so she nipped in the house while they're out and they came back just in time to scare her off. She managed to pick up her phone, apparently, and then leave it on the kitchen table, so she *still* doesn't know the charges have been dropped. No one can get in touch with her, and she's off on the run again. It's full alert.

'We got to help,' said Rob, the poor star-struck loon.

'Maiden in distress,' said Frankie. And he looked at

me and winked, and half nodded towards Rob, who was rushing about getting his gear ready.

Oh. Right. Frankie nodded and waggled his eyebrows. I get it. Rob to the rescue.

'You want us to come and help, Juggernaut?' asked Frankie, but Rob shook his head.

'No, she knows me and Chris. She trusts us.'

Trusts us? The bloke who pulled her kecks down? The other bloke who was going to get her locked up forever for stamping on his nads? (As far as she knew, anyway.) You must be joking. Still, I went along with it, partly to help Rob and partly because I have my own reasons for wanting to get in touch with Billie Trevors.

Give you a clue. Death growl. Gettit?

A girl singer. It has to be.

PART 4

Kill All Enemies

Rob

I wanted to be the one to find her. Why not? Everything had been going my way lately. Things can happen. Dreams can come true. I am living proof that you must never, ever give up hope.

We went round the park a couple of times. Nothing. I asked everyone we saw, but no one had seen her. We bumped into Hannah doing the rounds as well with a man and woman, who turned out to be Billie's carers. They hadn't seen her either. It looked like she'd given us the slip. I thought we'd missed our chance – but then we did this shortcut Chris knew round behind some shrubs and . . .

'Deathgrowl at three o'clock,' said Chris. And there she was, lying on a bench, tucked away behind some bushes and stuff. You wouldn't have noticed it being there at all, but Chris knew his way around.

'Ring Hannah,' I told him, and I ran off to get her. I heard Chris behind me calling me to wait – no way was I going to wait! I wanted to be first there. I wanted to be the one to tell her it was all right.

'Billie!' I yelled. She heard me coming and she sat up as I got close. I should have thought, but I had something to say to her, and nothing on this earth was going to stop me.

She got off the bench as I came up to her, and I tried to speak, but I was so excited and I'd run so fast I was out of breath. I stood there like an idiot, puffing and panting and trying to speak and not getting it out. She looked at me like I was some kind of moron and started to walk away, and I thought, *I'm not going to lose my chance now!*

I didn't think. I didn't know what she'd just been through. I grabbed out at her and pulled her round and I pulled her up to me and gave her a big Roly Poly love.

Bang! She went off in my arms. Suddenly I was staggering backwards and she was screaming in my face.

'No, Billie,' I said. I dodged down backwards and twisted out of the way – And then – there was a knife in her hand. It just came from nowhere. I never even saw her get it out.

'Billie, no!' I said. My voice sounded like she was just nicking chips off my plate. Then Chris shouted, 'Billie, no!' really loud, and I realized then, she really was going to stab me. Her face had gone red, her teeth were bared like a dog's and she was shaking like she was having some kind of breakdown. Her eyes had gone black. It wasn't Billie any more.

'We dropped the charges,' shouted Chris. 'Billie!'

I don't think she even heard him. I had to do something. I opened my mouth and . . .

'Billie,' I said. '. . . Will you go out with me?'

'What?'

I think I was almost as surprised as she was. But there – I'd said it now. 'Will you go out with me? I fancy you. Go on, Billie, please. What do you say?'

It was a stupid thing to say, I expect. It was almost as stupid as diving in and making a grab for her. But it got through to her. She looked at me, then she looked at the knife in her hand as if she'd never seen it before. She took a step backwards.

'What?' she said again.

'Billie,' said Chris. 'Drop the knife.'

She looked at him. She looked so confused.

'We're your mates,' he said. 'You don't need to fight us.'

Billie stared at him, then at me. I nodded. And then, slowly, she let her arm drop down . . .

There was a shout. It was Hannah running towards us. There was that couple following her, running as fast as they could, a string of them across the park.

'Give me the knife, Billie,' I said. 'They don't have to see that,' I said. She handed it over and I put it in my pocket. Her face creased up. She started to cry.

'Oh, Billie,' I said. 'Can I hug you now? Just a hug.'

And she gave this little nod, this tiny little nod. I came up to her, slowly this time, and she put her arms round me, and I put my arms round her. I hugged her and she hugged me back. She started to shake a bit, and then there she was, crying on my shoulder like a little kid.

Hannah

I came running up. Barbara had been shouting, 'Wait!' all the way, but I was that far gone. All that jogging pays off sometimes. There they were, the terrible triplets. Chris standing to one side, and Billie and Rob, wrapped up together. She was in his arms, crying her heart out. I was going to push them all to one side and just run in and give her a hug. But there he was doing it for me.

I came to a halt next to them.

'There, love,' I said. 'There, love. We're all here, aren't we?' She looked at me over his shoulder, and she tried to smile. Then Barbara came huffing up behind, her and Dan, and they ground to a halt too. There we stood, all four of us, watching Billie cry. In a moment she pushed Rob away. She came over to me and gave me a kiss. Then she went to Barbara and put her arms round her and just stood there hugging her.

Barbara looked astonished. She held her tight. 'You're coming home, Billie, right now,' she said firmly. Billie nodded. Barbara glanced at me, and I nodded, and she led her off, still crying. I watched after her. And – I was a little hurt, if I'm to be honest. There I was waiting for her, and it was Rob and Barbara she turned to. But – she'd done it, hadn't she? She'd let them in. She wasn't even trying to hide those tears. Barbara will take care of her. And Rob – well, he was so far from her usual crowd, he might have been another species. He was a nice lad. Since when did Billie end up crying on the shoulder of a nice lad?

She was learning.

There now, I thought. *Maybe we're getting there after all.*

Rob

So I'm walking home and I'm thinking, *Life cannot get any better than this.* I have everything I ever wanted. I actually had the courage to ask Billie to go out with me. I don't think she's going to say yes. But you never know. At least I tried.

And then I get to the door. And I remember.

It's been two weeks since I came back from Mum's. I was certain he was going to go yesterday, but it turned out the car had been up for its MOT. It'd been given the all-clear in the afternoon. Today was Sunday. He'd be thinking how she'd be at home, most like. He'd go today, surely.

Yeah. Today. It has to be.

I touched the bonnet of the car. I do that every day I come home.

It was warm.

It was all quiet in the house. Philip was in the kitchen cooking something. The door was open. He nodded as I went past.

'All right, Rob?' he said.

'OK,' I said. And I thought, *It's cool! He's not gone. Wow.* I felt good again. I went upstairs. Davey was in. I could hear music coming out of his room.

'All right, Davey,' I shouted. I went into my room and put the computer on and waited for it to start up. I was thinking that Philip was a bit odd down there. I don't know, something about the way he looked at me.

The computer got going. I stood up and I went to Davey's room.

'Davey?' I called – not too loud in case Philip heard. 'Davey? You OK?' He still didn't answer. I rattled the doorknob, but he'd locked it. 'What's going on?' I called, although there was no reason to think anything was going on. He often locks the door.

Philip turned up at the bottom of the stairs.

'Leave the lad alone, you big monkey. He's tired,' he said. So I went back into my room and faffed around a bit. But then I crept back out and tried his door again.

'Davey,' I called softly.

'What?' he said, and his voice was a bit off, you know what I mean, a bit off?

'Let me in,' I said.

'Go away,' he said.

And I thought, for no reason, *I'm not having this.*

So I turned the doorknob and I leaned very quietly, but with all my weight, against the door. It was only a little bolt and it just gave. I could hear the screws pull out. Davey was lying on the bed with his face away from me.

'Davey?' I said, and I went over to him and grabbed him by the shoulder and pulled him, and I could see at once that some bastard had hit him. The whole side of his face was bright red. Then we had this tussle where I was pulling at him to get a look, going, 'Let me see, let me see,' and he was pulling away and trying to hide it, going, 'Leave me alone, leave me alone.' Some bullying bastard had really done a job on him – his eye was out here and his face was red and he'd been crying.

I was steaming.

'Who did this?' I said. 'Who was it, who did this to you? Was it Riley? Who did it?'

And he was going, 'Leave me alone, leave me alone, stop it, stop it,' and cracking up and crying as he spoke. And then suddenly he turned round, and I could see the full thing then – bloody nose, fat lip, black eye, bright red skin – and he hissed it right in my face.

'Why are you asking me that? You know who did it! You know who did it. You bloody know!'

He turned away and started crying proper then. I went back into my room. I sat down and played on the PC for a bit – I don't know how long, maybe a few minutes, maybe longer. Then I got up suddenly and I ran downstairs. I ran down, before I had time to think. Before I had time to bottle out.

Philip knew. He came out into the hall and he had his belt folded double in his hand.

'Think you're ready for it, do you, then?' he said.

'I think I am,' I said. I went for him, but he stopped me in my tracks with that belt – *whack!* – right round the face. God, it stung. He got a couple of blows in with the belt while I was stunned, but I pushed in close, shoved him backwards and swung at him, a big old round swing. He stepped round me, but the hall wasn't wide enough and I caught him on the side of the face, a deflected blow. It was my first hit. He put his hand to his jaw and smiled and shook his head.

'Is that it?' he said. 'Is that all you have?'

I got another one in; he got one in on my nose. My eyes were watering so much I couldn't see much. I got a good one on him in the stomach; I could hear the air go out of him. He threw the belt away then, when he knew it was fists or nowt. We tussled up and down the hallway and then he tripped up and staggered and I got a good one, right on the side of his neck. Down he went, down on to the hallway carpet. And you know what I did then? Do you want to know?

I kicked that fucker all the way up the hallway to the front door. He kept trying to get up, but I just took his legs from under him every time and started again. *Bang, bang bang*, all the way up the hall to the door.

'Stop, stop,' he started going. But I didn't. Eventually I had him up against the front door and I still didn't stop. I just carried on until I heard Davey behind me calling.

'That's enough, Rob,' he yelled. 'It's enough.'

I stopped. I stood there panting.

'Do you want a go?' I asked Davey, but he shook his head.

I turned to Philip, down there on the floor. I was on a roll. Everything was getting better and better. Nothing could stop me. Now this. The hardest thing. I'd done it. I'd broken him and his shit spell and I was finally turning back into myself.

I still had my coat on. There was something heavy in my pocket. I patted it and there it was – Billie's knife. I took it out. I looked at it in my hand and I thought, *I could end this now. I could stop it forever – for Mum and for Davey and for me*. He was already moving to get up, but he stopped when he saw the knife. He looked at it and then he looked at me and I looked back. He was going to get up. I could stop him. If you do that to someone, if you stab them, they're going to be scared of you forever.

There was a long pause. Philip was panting, looking up at me. And then – then he smiled.

'You haven't got the guts, have you?' he said.

'You'd love that, wouldn't you?' I said. I didn't know what I was going to say; it just came out. 'If I did that, you'd have won, because then I'd be just like you. But you haven't, and I'm not. So why don't you just fuck off out and get on with your miserable, sad, bullying little life, before I kick your sorry arse through that door.' I turned round to Davey, who was standing on the stairs.

'Right, Davey?' I said.

'Right, Rob,' he said.

I turned round and walked off. I said, 'Twat,' over my shoulder – just so he knew. I went upstairs back to my room.

Way to go, Robbie, I said to myself. And then – then I got on with my homework.

Chris

It was science. Wikes. For once in my life, I was early for class. I was waiting outside the classroom near the window by the fire extinguisher. No one knew it yet, but this was going to be my last day at school.

We had our first gig the other day. Kill All Enemies – Full Speed to Hell. I put out loads of leaflets, but hardly any of mine turned up. It was embarrassing. Alex came, skulked about a bit, then left.

'Didn't you like it?' I texted him.

'Like doesn't even come into it,' he said. And ever since then I've been some kind of pariah. I've joined another club. Or, more like, I've joined another species. I've known these people since primary school and all I had to do was change my musical tastes, grow my hair, put on a leather jacket and – bingo! – there they're not.

And it was a great gig. Billie came in with her death growl. Her and Frankie on vocals – what a team! I don't know if she'll stay, but fingers crossed. I was on stage for the last number, joining in on vocals. I can't sing, but the guys insisted.

'Shoulder to shoulder. Brothers,' said Frankie.

All their mates were there – forty or fifty of them. And about three of mine. New mates, new life. The eBay shop is trading again. I have the band. Things are definitely looking up. Except for one thing . . .

School. No time, no inclination – no go. I thought my parents were on the verge of giving it up, but would you believe it, they'd actually found another way in – with the help of sneaky Hannah. Dyslexia. Apparently the previous tests I did were all wrong.

I wasn't surprised. Reading and writing have always been a pain in the neck for me. I sit there and sweat at it, while everyone else just sails away. The trouble is they were four years too late.

They had it all worked out, of course. The school was onside. They'd found a specialist for me to go to. Oh, there were plenty of apologies. They'd let me down, the school had let me down – but the end result was just the same as before. Work. Work, work and more work.

I didn't say anything. Why bother? I'd heard it all before. I knew exactly how to foil their foolish plans before they even got off the ground. It was going to take some balls, that's all. I might have trouble writing stuff, but balls – I have them in plenty.

From where I stood by the window, I could see the box of coloured pens sitting on Wikes's desk, waiting to be put to work destroying young minds. Alex and Mickey and a couple of the others looked at me curiously as they walked past into the classroom – all trotting in willingly, like lambs to the slaughter. Me? I had the means of my deliverance right there, hanging next to me on the wall by the window.

I didn't have long to wait. Wikes came round the corner into the corridor – and – great! He had the dep head with him. Perfect.

I was going to go out in a blaze of glory.

I waited until they got good and close. I didn't want to blow it by letting them get away. I gave them a little smile as they approached. I felt shy now it came down to it. I mean, they had no idea what it was about. Neither did I, really, except I knew it was for Rob and for Frankie and for Billie and for me too, and for anyone else who has to spend years and years and years having to do stuff they hate, just because no one has the imagination to let you find something else to do. I hoiked the fire extinguisher out of its cradle when they were about four metres away. They stopped in their tracks.

'What do you think you're doing, Trent?' barked Wikes. The dep head just ogled me, like he couldn't believe it.

'No,' he said.

'But yes,' I said. I lifted it up, pulled out the pin and . . .

There was nowhere to hide. They turned and ran so I had to chase them up the corridor, just so they knew there was no mistake. It was them I was after. I got 'em good. I got ’em so good, they started slithering around on the foamy goo and ended up on their bums, nowhere to go, nowhere to hide, covered in white foam like a pair of penguins in batter. I emptied the extinguisher and then I swung it round and chucked it through the window. *Crash!* I love the sound of breaking glass. Then I turned round and I walked out of that useless dump forever.

Acknowledgements

The idea behind this book was what you might call 'found fiction' – starting with real people and the real stories behind them. Since those first interviews, of course, the whole thing has been changed . . . characters have been developed and merged, others invented, situations removed, blown up, turned around . . . in short, it has been fictionalized. But I hope that many of the people I spoke to when I was putting the book together can find traces of themselves in these pages.

As a result, there are a great many people to thank. I had a major advantage writing this one, as the project was first commissioned by Channel Four, with a view to making TV out of it. Lime Pictures, the production company, provided a researcher to help me, which made a huge difference to the collection of material. My thanks then to C4 for the original commission, even if it got no further than script stage, and especially to Tony Wood who sold the idea to them in the first place. Also to Tim Compton who script-edited the early stages, and most especially to

Natalie Grant, the researcher, who helped so much in the early stages. I wonder how many of them you recognize, Nat?

A big thank-you to Kaye Tew from MMU, the first person I spoke to, and her son, Callum.

I talked to a great many people at PRUs, care homes and other organizations around the North West. Organizations of this kind vary enormously in this country, but along with a few grim ones I came across some wonderful places, staffed by people who were truly inspirational. I'm thinking of Karen and Jenny in Didsbury, Lisa and Joelle in the Wirral. Also Rob Loach in Harrogate and everyone in the wonderful PRU in Blackburn. Fresh fruit in every room and flowers in the corridor – so much that I much admired.

As for the young people I spoke to, and who impressed me so much – special thanks to Jamie, Jamie, Matt and Jay from Kill All Enemies for spending so much time telling me their stories – and not least for letting me pinch the name of their band for my book. These guys turned themselves into kind and generous people by sheer strength of mind – and through music. And of course, special thanks to Bobby-Joe – a true warrior and an inspiration to many people.

There are a great many more – I could go on for pages. If you're not here it's for one reason only; among so many wonderful stories, from staff and students alike, you can't use them all in just one book. I could write three more and not repeat myself once.

I'd like to thank all the people who helped with the actual manuscript: Mary Byre for her excellent suggestions, and all the good folk at Puffin – Sarah, my editor, and Wendy Tse and Samantha Mackintosh for their work on timelines and for getting the words in the right order.

Finally, many, many thanks to Anita, my partner, who spent days and days reading and re-reading the book, editing, advising and coming up with some marvellous ideas when I was going word-blind. She was tireless, ruthless and uncompromising, and *Kill All Enemies* wouldn't be half the book it is without her.

Thanks to you all – I hope you like the book.